*Of
Friends and
Others*

Other novels by J. A. Sanborn

The Lost Cipher
The Orion Factor
Death Comes to Ely
The Stillwater Incident

**All books above are available in Kindle eBook edition
or soft cover at Amazon.com**

Copyright © 2017 Dr. Jon A. Sanborn,
Of Friends and Others

Swift River Publishing, LLC
P.O. Box 30965
Savannah, GA 31410
swiftriverpublishing.com
swiftriverpublishing@gmail.com

ISBN: 978-0-9968082-8-6

OF FRIENDS AND OTHERS

LXXI
"The Moving Finger writes; and having writ,
Moves on: nor all thy Piety nor Wit
Shall lure it back to cancel half a Line,
Nor all thy Tears wash out a Word it."

From the Rubaiyat of Omar Kayyàm, 1120 A.C.E

It is better to be deceived by one's friends than to deceive them. *Goethe*

*Of Friends
And Others*

*a novel
by
J. A. Sanborn*

Chapter One

The story I am about to relate is true. You need to know this before you read another line. Many details of this narrative have come to me over several years from family, friends, and from my own experiences, although time has made some memories factual, or so I believe, even though others may not agree.

Before I get ahead of myself with this account, a few things of importance need to be explained. First, my family consisted of my mother and me living in the city of Augusta. I will share more about Mom and me later, but for now, you should know that I was fatherless, my mother was without a mate, and times were hard for us.

At the time of this narrative, Augusta had a population of nearly thirty thousand citizens having a mix of white-collar professionals and blue-collar workers who form the backbone of the City's success. In other words, it was a traditional type of New England city.

The present city is what I call a "low" city with metes and bounds encompassing nearly twenty square miles in area. The city boasts of having a central business district where commercial and business enterprises operate with no building higher than four floors.

Institutional memory of the city's founding is based on Royal Grants of land by Great Britain's King George I to several noteworthy men of the time. One of these men was James Glendale who settled in this area around 1710.

Subsequent existing early land deeds and their

references indicate that the Glendale family owned nearly the entire region of the present-day city of Augusta along with clear title to the three-thousand-acre lake known for years as Glendale's Pond as its name appeared on old maps. Around a hundred years ago, Augusta annexed the entire lake area. Later it was renamed Glendale Lake to satisfy the lake's water-side residents.

The lake and all its surrounding acreage are in the northeast part of the city, which not surprisingly, is dubbed the Glendale District in keeping with the lake's moniker. Money, masses of it, has moved into the serene atmosphere of the area since annexation.

Substantial homes ring the lake front. I say substantially because they were beautifully built, large and well maintained by their wealthy owners and heirs. Anyone, who is anyone, seems to have built or purchased a place on the lake.

My mother and I did not live in the lake area, as you may have supposed at this point. My mother, Anita L. Connor, named me, Robert, after my father whom I never met. Mom told me that my birth weight was only six and a half pounds. She said that I was so weak that the doctors didn't believe I would live.

My mother, prior to the time of my birth, was a woman of eighteen with a slim figure, as pictures in an old album show. She weighed about one hundred pounds, had dark brown hair, a petite nose, and brown eyes. For a young child of four, in love with his mother, she seemed to be much taller than her five-foot four-inch stature. She was very attractive because even at a young age, I noticed that men would turn their heads when she was in the area.

As you may suspect, I have fond memories of my mother. When she was baking or cooking some meal for us, she would have me bring up a chair to help. She spent many hours reading stories to me.

As for my looks, I was the infant whose face was one that only my mother could love. She had shown to me several baby pictures; I didn't see how she could love me. But she did, devoting her energy to make me comfortable and feel loved.

I had inherited her beautiful brown hair and eyes, but not her nose. Mine seemed to grow faster than Pinocchio's and my ears could be described as stunted wind catchers. The only redeeming feature I had was my surging height. By the time I was nine years old, I was taller than my mother

During my early years, my mother had told me that my father died several months before I was born. She had married at a young age, eighteen, and been pregnant with me when he died. She told me that I was a "honeymoon baby." The expression was a mystery to me, because I didn't know what a "honeymoon baby" was. I asked, but my mother never explained what it meant.

When I was older, I asked her about my grandparents, her mother and father, and my dad's parents. She said that they had fallen out of touch, because they lived so far away. That didn't make any sense to me, but she said that that was the way it was in a tone I dreaded. When I pushed for answers, I could see tears forming in her eyes. It was her sadness, which stopped me from asking any more questions about my grandparents. It would be years before she could develop the courage to tell me the truth.

My mother kept a single, faded, colored photograph of my father. It was always perched on the maple table placed next to the only sofa we ever owned. In the photograph, a young man was dressed in an Army uniform posed with a rifle in his right hand. A Quonset hut with its familiar tubular shape provided the background. The entrance to the hut bore stenciling in large letters which was partially blocked by my father's image such that only the word "Fort" was visible.

I could see that he had a gentle face graced with beautiful brown eyes, bushy brown eyebrows, and a small nose. His mouth was frozen with a smile which gave me the impression that, perhaps, he was hiding some secret. In my self-centered world at the time, I wondered, in my self-centered world of thought, if I were the secret.

As I grew older, I noticed other features about the man in the photograph. For one, his ears were tightly clasped to his head, unlike mine. My ears stretched out from my head like they were meant for an aerial lift off. Mom told me that when I was a baby, she had tried taping my ears to my head hoping to make them flatter. Apparently, an old folklore tale had offered her such advice. For us, it did not work. I thought that perhaps my father's mother had better luck

4

than mine. To this day, my ears stand out.

Until I was ten, I believed my father had died in some undefined accident. One day when I pressed Mom for an answer, she told me that he had died in a war. She didn't say which war, but I figured that it must have been in the Korean War, since I was born in 1952. It was on July fourth, to be more specific.

Having seen other photographs of soldiers, my father's snapshot was missing some important details I expected it to have. His Army uniform had no stripes on his sleeves. So, I thought, Dad must have been a Private, maybe a draftee. Also, the rifle didn't seem right in the picture.

Later, I read about the war. The rifle, a 1903 Springfield, my father posed with was not Army issue in that war. A few were modified for sniper use. So, the rifle my father had was only for training.

I asked Mom when the picture was taken. She said it was when he had completed his basic training. He had been sent to the war shortly after that.

I had heard somewhere that soldiers who died in wars were given medals. Had any medals been presented to him? Mom said that she didn't know. I asked her if she had any pictures of my father with his medals. She said there were none.

I resented that war, in which we fought people we didn't even know, had taken my father's life. I didn't know the reason then, but these days I think it must be a fatal flaw in our genetic makeup.

For reasons which I did not understand at the time, my mother had kept nothing personal of my father. For certain, the Army would have sent her a letter or telegram about his death. There was no letter of condolence, nor a telegram: "We are sorry to report that your husband has been reported missing and presumed dead."

When I asked her, Mom said that they had been lost, but she never explained how. Apparently even their marriage certificate had been one of the "lost" vital papers.

I asked many questions for which my mother gave the impression that she had no answers. Eventually, my mother's impatience began to show, so I stopped asking about my father and other details about their lives. At one time, I started to believe that the photograph was one my mother had simply picked up somewhere, but that was too harsh as I later found out. To this day, however, I have not been able to find facts about my father's life. He remains a mystery.

Living in Augusta, life was not easy for my mother in many ways. When I was young, I became aware that women we met would stop talking to each other while we passed by. Then they would face each other and smile a kind of smile that revealed they knew something embarrassing about us, but didn't want us to hear them gossiping. I asked Mom why they acted that way, but she said she didn't know. Now, I understand that she was aware of the affront, but was too embarrassed to tell me. It was simply her way to shield me from a cruel world.

As I said, life was not easy for us. With a small child to rear, my mother had no income to support us, so we had been on charity rolls for as long as I could remember. Because she had no saleable skills, my mother had no alternative but to seek assistance from the city.

Back then, people were looked down upon for taking money from the good citizens of any city. People like my mother were considered really not worthy of the citizens' largess. Support money was given stingily and it came with loss of dignity for the person receiving it.

The apartment, which the city rented for us, was one located in a building indirectly connected to an operating dairy farm. Originally, the building must have been the farm owner's home, but over the years the house had been divided into several studios, if you could call them that, and let to tenants. A gravel driveway separated our house from the large whitewashed barn, which was the main building for the dairy farm.

Our apartment was small, very small. It had a kitchen area with an ugly sink and no counter space to speak of. An ancient gas range, which required many matches to light, sat next to a wheezing refrigerator to keep the temperature cool. An oak table sized for three people sat against a wall. Three mismatched chairs in various states of needed repair completed the setting. The table was obviously a hand-me-down from some source known only to the landlord.

The small living room was furnished with our sofa and side table holding my father's photograph. I slept on a pull-down bed shakily affixed to one wall of the living room. My clothes were stacked on three shelves unevenly tacked to the wall opposite my bed. This room was what the British would call a bedsit, where a straight back chair in front of my small desk completed the décor.

Sometime in the past, the landlord must have gotten a deal on some garish paisley wallpaper. He had the entire apartment's walls pasted from ceiling to mopboard with it.

My mother had the only real bedroom. It had a double sized bed with a mattress sporting a pronounced sag in the middle. Its age probably exceeded two decades. The landlord must have bought several straight back chairs because the mirror image of my chair sat in her room. My mother also had a small writing desk situated on the far wall and an old treadle Singer sewing machine next to her bed. Her bedroom had a small closet for her wardrobe and a tiny dresser for her personals.

Still, our apartment kept the rain and snow from our heads, providing some warmth in winter but also stifling heat in summer. The barnyard smells in summer prevented us from opening any windows to get fresh air. Worse, the absence of screens would let in swarms of flies to constantly flit about the apartment spreading their filth.

The exterior of the house needed a coat of paint for years becoming an eyesore to the area. But who were we to think that we rated anything finer from the good citizens?

The old welfare system sometimes led to exploitation of people in such straits. Back then, a few dollars were stingily given with many stipulations.

I remember that once a month, Percy Lovejoy, the city's welfare manager, would come to our house to inspect and comment on our living standards and to deliver our money for the coming few weeks. Percy did not spend as much time at the other "assistance" tenant's apartments as he did at ours, but then the only good-looking woman in the whole building was my mother.

As I grew older, I thought it was strange that whenever Percy arrived, he and my mom would go into her room to discuss the money he brought.

Once, I asked my mother why they needed to talk in her room. He had instructions, she said, which outlined what my mother needed to do to keep us on the welfare system. Mom said that I should never have to hear details about the money given to us, so they went there for privacy. It was such a small apartment that it made sense to me.

She told me that Mister Lovejoy was being very kind to us by giving us extra money, but it had to be a secret because he might be fired if his boss found out. And so, I was sworn to secrecy.

Sometimes I would listen at the door but most of the time the only things I heard were their voices talking softly, but I could never make out the words.

The apartment rent was paid by the city to a Mister Jeremiah Hubbard, the landlord, who also came by frequently to be sure that we were taking good care of his property. Mom had to speak with Mister Hubbard quite often to explain why and how I had damaged something in our luxurious apartment. He would speak harshly to my mother, yelling at her and me.

I did not tell my mother that I had another secret. There were days when my mother went shopping. She had to walk downtown to the nearest grocery store or whatever to shop, usually leaving me at the apartment when there was no school.

On a few occasions while she was out, Mister Hubbard came to the house. He had a key and went to her bedroom. He spent time to snooping through her desk and closet. I knew that if I told my mother, she would call the police, and Hubbard would throw us out onto the street.

Hubbard and Lovejoy were evil. Their treatment and disrespect of my mother were disgusting, but she never complained. Mom was a loving mother who did whatever she felt necessary to survive and protect me.

It was only when I was older that I understood how much my mother sacrificed. It incensed me, and as a naïve child, I vowed to punish those two men. What we did not realize was that their treatment of us was being carefully watched. It turned out that I would be spared my Oath, but that comes later in this story.

Chapter Two

As I have mentioned earlier, the house we lived in was adjacent to a huge barn of an operating dairy farm. The seventy-acre farm itself consisted of several necessary buildings and structures clustered near our house. In addition to the large barn housing the milking equipment, hay loft, and the animals at night, there were two ensilage silos and a large garage for storage of large equipment, trucks and tractors, so important to the operation of a successful farm.

There was also a small cottage, if I may call it that, along the dirt road giving access to the pastures. It was occupied by an old man who had worked many years on the farm. Later, I would learn that his name was Janek Gulden who helped the farmer with the morning and evening milking chores.

The farmer also rented acreage outside of the city limits for hay and corn. This farm was the last remaining one operating within the city limits of Augusta. In fact, in the future of Augusta, there would be no others. The City Council passed a zoning ordinance which permitted this farm to operate until it shut down. After that, all the property owned and used by the farm would be re-zoned from agriculture to residential use.

The dairy farm was owned by Mister Hepburn who also resided in the house where our apartment was located. He was a large man having broad shoulders, a thin waist, and stood more than six feet tall.

He had a warm smile and pleasant face, although it was somewhat hidden with a trim red beard. His red hair was in a state of perpetual barbering need with tufts visible along the edges of his baseball hat, which continually sported the New York Yankee's logo. His blue eyes and warm smile made a person feel comfortable.

His work overalls were clean, I imagine when he put them on in the morning, but at the end of the day, they showed numerous splatters and stains when the chores were done. I thought that he must spend hours washing his clothes.

When I was seven years old, I asked my mother if I could go to the barn and talk to Mister Hepburn. She said that she would have to talk to him first, which she did. The rule was that I would be permitted to go to the barn after school when I had finished my homework. I didn't know it then, but Mister Hepburn was to help shape my early years and become one of my most sincere, trustworthy, dependable friends.

Mister Hepburn's primary farm animals included twenty-five Holsteins to care for and milk with a small number of calves nurtured until the age when they were sold for veal. At first, I gave little thought to the calves but as the years passed at the farm, I felt a sense of sorrow for the little creatures and their fate.

Along with the milking herd, there was a small flock of chickens providing eggs and many barn cats who kept the mouse population in check.

By the time I got to the barn each day, Mister Hepburn had already prepared the stanchion area for each cow. He had shoveled soiled wood sawdust into the gutter behind each stanchion and had swept down the area where each animal would be for milking. After that, he had shoveled the aromatic manure/sawdust mix into a cart, which he wheeled out of the barn to an open shed, located in the outer yard. It was there that the evil smelling stuff was piled and left to age.

In the Spring, another chore would be to hitch the tractor to the manure spreader, load the spreader from the pile and spread it over the grazing pastures. Good fertilizer, he always said.

Having finished that chore, Mister Hepburn would shovel down a fresh, thick layer of delightfully smelling wood sawdust to make a bed where the cows (his babies) would eventually lie down after feeding and the milking chores were done.

Then it was time to bring in the cows. I watched the daily ritual as he went out to the pasture gate to call. Mister Hepburn had a deep voice and would shout "Come Boss, Come Boss." When they heard his voice, the animals would start lumbering toward him.

Mister Hepburn said this was the easiest chore of the day because the cows would start to meander from the pasture area to the gate without his call. After a day in the meadow, their filling udders signaled them it was time to head to the barn for milking.

Once inside the barn, they knew exactly what to do. They would go to a stanchion and put their heads through them. Then Mister Hepburn would lock the stanchion. In front of each stanchion, he had already placed broken bales of fresh hay for them to eat during milking. Each station had a drinking water system, which refilled as the cow drank.

With each animal in place, Mister Hepburn or Mister Gulden would gently wash the cow's udder and teats with a warm solution of water laced with a gentle antibiotic.

Sometimes he or Mister Gulden would playfully hand milk a cow and spray the milk into the open mouth of one of the barn cats. Soon many of the cats would come running over for their treat.

If one of Mister Hepburn's "babies" had a damaged teat, he would gently milk her by hand and then apply Bag Balm to help heal the sore.

For the other cows, Mister Hepburn would attach the milking machine to the cow's teats and milking would proceed. When the milking was done, the milk was poured into stainless milk cans, which were put immediately into large, low refrigerators that were half filled with cold water to await the morning pickup. His last chore involved thoroughly cleaning the milking machines with hot water to be ready for the next milking in the morning before letting the cows out to graze in the field. Mister Hepburn told me that his milking schedule was twice a day, morning and evening, but that other farms milked three times.

One day, late in the fall, Mister Hepburn asked me if I would like a job after school to help with the chores. When I asked, my mother wasn't very happy about the idea, but she finally agreed after Mister Hepburn told her I would be doing only the light chores. He would make sure I would be done by five o'clock in time for supper. He told my mother he could only pay me a dollar an hour.

I think my mom knew he was lonely and needed someone to talk to, so she made it a point to spend some time with him after the chores were done. He would come to our apartment and have a glass of wine with my mother. They talked about many things, but it was boring so I usually didn't listen to them.

One day, Mister Hepburn asked me if the visits from Percy and Mister Hubbard discontinued. I told him that neither Lovejoy nor Hubbard was visiting my mother anymore. I asked if he knew why the visits had stopped. He said that he had had "a word" with each of them, and that they had taken the hint.

I asked Mister Hepburn if he knew why they paid visits to my mom. He said that they had reasons which were not good. I wasn't aware of what happens between men and women yet, so I didn't understand exactly what he implied. But then again, I already knew their visits were not good for my mother, whatever their intent.

Mister Hepburn told me that if we were going to get along, that I should call him, Roy. He introduced me to his helper, Mister Gulden who told me to call him Janek.

And so, I began my first job. The first task was to climb the vertical ladder up to the hayloft where the warmth and smell of the hay surrounded me. Then, I dragged five bales to the loft opening and dropped five bales of hay down to Janek. Next, we cut the baling strings, broke up the bales, and placed the hay into the feeding troughs for Roy's "babies."

As I grew older and stronger, I could help Roy with the more strenuous chores. I would do the dirty work of shoveling out the manure gutters. For me it was backbreaking work, but I loved it. I grew to love the smells of a dairy farm, which clung to my clothes and body. My mother, I know, did not have that same love of farm life for a variety of reasons, one of which was the need to wash my soiled, smelly clothes each day.

Nevertheless, I felt a great sense of accomplishment. I was becoming a farmer. Helping to care for animals was an empowering feeling for a young boy. Roy told me that farming built character in a person. I believe that to this day.

I learned to throw a large leather strap across the back of a cow and hook the strap end to the milking machine, which was a stainless-steel tank with four teat cups affixed to the tank by rubber hoses. I would connect the hose from the tank to a connector of the suction supply line. Then I would place a cup onto each teat.

When the milk was exhausted from the udder, I removed the tank and poured the milk into a stainless milk can, which Roy or Janek would place into the refrigerator.

I would explain all the work I was learning to do to my mother. Mom did not like me to use words as tits, which Roy did when he referred to the cows' teats.

"Don't use that kind of language, Robert," she reprimanded. I didn't use those words around her anymore, but Roy and I did, chuckling at Mom's prudishness.

Roy taught me many things about farming and life. He was there when I needed someone to help me understand things of the world, which my mother found difficult to do. Roy often spoke about my mother in a way that made me realize that, in a way, he had feelings for her. Mom said that Roy was very lonely. I could tell that he had eyes for her, and that she had them for him.

My mother always insisted that she and I have a sit-down dinner after I returned from my "work." My mother invited Roy to dinner once a week on Friday night. Of course, when Roy was invited, dinner was delayed until Roy had finished his chores and cleaned up.

This dinner on Friday ritual continued for several years. Sometimes on Saturday evenings, the three of us would go to the movies at the local drive-in theater.

Other times, my mother and Roy would go alone. I hoped something would develop between them. I wanted Roy to be my father.

About once a month, Roy would also dine with us on Wednesday and they would go somewhere after we had eaten. Those nights I would stay home.

Kids at school were mean and said that Mom and Roy were doing "it." I had several fights trying to shut the kids up, but I never won. I didn't know what "it" was, but I knew I couldn't ask either Mom or Roy. Later I knew that they had become intimate even though, at the time, I wasn't sure what intimacy was.

I told my mother that it would be okay if she married Roy since she seemed to enjoy spending time with him. He would come to visit her and sometimes she would go to his apartment.

I hoped and believed that they would marry so he could be my dad, but it did not happen. His homey visits continued until one day my mother announced that we would be leaving Augusta. I was devastated.

By that time, I was nearly twelve and the idea of moving crushed me because this house was the only one I had ever known, and Roy had been the only man who had treated me well. I considered him to be my father. Nevertheless, Mom said we had to go and that was that.

I knew that Mom had been taking courses at the local junior college and felt she was ready for a real job. She had applied for a position at a manufacturing company located in Bards Crossing, a small town I'd never heard of.

When I went to see Roy, I had tears in my eyes. Roy seemed to have moist eyes also as we hugged and said our goodbyes. I had come to love that man as a father and a friend. He told me that my mother was a fine person and he was sorry to see us leave. He had asked her to marry him, but she said she needed to be independent and lead her life the way she wanted.

I realized that she probably did love Roy. He had been kind to us and, I think would have made a fine husband for Mom, but she had things to prove to herself and the family that had abandoned her. The cost was high as I look back on her decision, but I realize that all decisions have consequences, which are not always easy to see at the time. It was only later in my life that I really understood what she had been enduring to keep us going. Mom had developed the confidence to set out on her own and we had to move, whether I liked it or not.

I did extract one commitment from my mother. I would be allowed to return to Augusta and stay with Roy during the summer breaks from high school.

I need to tell you one more aspect about Roy before I describe the move to Bards Crossing.

I had asked Roy why he wasn't married. His answer surprised me. He said that he had been married for several years. Something terrible had happened. He and his wife had gone deer hunting in Canada, the other side of Lake Champlain when some cowboy from New York had mistakenly shot her. The cowboy had gotten "buck fever" and hastily fired. He had disobeyed a fundamental rule of firearms: "Do not fire at anything until you know what it is, and you mean to shoot it." Roy's wife died in his arms.

The police arrested the "hunter" but he retained a sharp lawyer, who got the manslaughter charge dropped. Roy was incensed by the injustice, Roy had lost the love of his life and the system did not care. Roy said that he never forgot the man.

When I told Roy how sorry I was, he said that life had a way of evening out these injustices. He told me that somehow, somewhere, incidents happen to right a system wrong. He said that life was serendipitous at times.

I asked him what he meant. His reply was that a person can't shoot what a person can't see. I again asked, but he only flashed his familiar warm smile. I started to ask another question, but he signaled the topic was done. I never spoke of it again to him.

Chapter Three

Looking back at our move from Augusta, it wasn't as grave as my adolescent mind thought it would be. As one door in my life closed, another opened. In Augusta, I wasn't shunned by classmates at school, but I wasn't welcomed into their homes either. Except for Roy, and to some extent, Janek, there were no friends, certainly no childhood friends. So, I did not expect anything to be different by moving to another town.

However, Bards Crossing turned out to be unlike Augusta in many ways. We had moved from a city to this one stop-light town located a hundred miles from Augusta, whose population at the time was about fifteen hundred. There were no indications that more people would be flocking to settle to this sleepy place anytime soon.

The school system had become regionalized the year we moved. Four towns made up the Regional School District, which included Lancaster and Bards Crossing with Millersville and Jasper completing the system. A new high school, Alice Day Regional High School, had been constructed in Lancaster.

Elementary education ended at the eighth-grade level. After an annual graduation ceremony, students rising into the ninth grade were now bussed to Lancaster, about ten miles away. Since I was a rising ninth grader, my next step was to the high school.

My mother had rented an old house located on East Main Street, situated next to the Congregational Church.

Every Sunday, Mom and I made the short walk to listen to the words of the minister expounding on the need to lead a saintly life to prepare for the afterlife. I thought it was enough work just to live now, much less worry about the hereafter, but his sermons had a lasting impact on me.

In Bards Crossing, I discovered my lineage, my true lineage, because of a serendipitous event which occurred. Shortly after moving in, we discovered that the movers had broken the frame of my father's picture. As a result, my father's photograph had slipped out of the frame and fallen to the floor.

Picking it up, I examined the back of the picture. The writing shocked me. It was endorsed "To Anita, With Love, Bob O'Dell."

"Mom, who is Bob O'Dell?" I asked indignantly. "You told me my father was Robert Connor."

Suddenly, tears began to run down her cheeks. Unknowingly, I had struck a deep nerve in her. It made me deeply embarrassed for hurting her, because my question had forced her into a place, which she did not want to go.

"It's okay, Mom," I said trying to stop my own tears, "You don't have to tell me."

"No, Robbie, it is about time we talked."

Mom sat down to share painful details of our lives which she had put off doing for so long.

"Robert, please sit down. You are old enough for the truth."

The only times she called me Robert was when I was

being scolded for some reason, or she had something serious on her mind, so I knew this was arduous for her.

"This is difficult for me to say to you, Robert. I have dreaded this moment since you were born. I am ashamed. I am ashamed to tell you that I have never been married," she said with tears streaming from her eyes.

"What? Does that mean I'm a bastard?" I asked.

"Don't ever say that about yourself, Robbie. It means nothing of the kind," Mom answered with anger in her voice. "You are as legitimate as any child that was ever born."

"Yes, but…"

"Let me explain some things. Bob O'Dell was a classmate whom I dated a few times in my last year of high school. He was nice to me, and I began to have warm feelings for him. He invited me to the senior prom. Afterward, we went to the prom party. A month later, school ended for us. We went to the all-night graduation party.

"You are fourteen, so I think you can understand what happened. We were two young kids who were thoughtless that night. What happened should not have happened and you were the result."

"So, you didn't really want me?"

"Oh, Robbie, I wanted you from the very first moment that I knew I was…"

"Why didn't you two get married?"

"O'Dell got scared, cold feet as they used to say. We

knew it was for the best. He had no earning skills. It would have been a marriage with many problems."

"What happened to him?"

"He left town sometime soon after. He didn't want me to have you, but that was out of the question. He wanted me to get an illegal abortion, but I could never do that. I wanted my baby. I wanted you. I was determined to keep you."

"Will he ever come to see me? Where is he today?" I asked.

"I don't really know. A classmate wrote me once that he had joined the Army. Sometime later, he sent the photograph. I have never heard from him again. At first, I was going to throw the photo out, but I kept it for you. I felt you should know, at least, how he looked."

"Mom, were you planning to go to college?"

"I was. I had been accepted to the state university and I planned to be a teacher. I loved science and wanted to teach that, but I had to decide once I found out I was pregnant. I tried to delay telling my parents for a couple of months, but eventually I had to. I was at the university and when I began to show, I admitted it to my roommate. She convinced me that I had to tell them. The sooner I did, the better.

"So, I withdrew from the college and went home to face the 'music.' I will tell you, Robbie, that the 'music' was very harsh. I gathered my clothes, some of my childhood treasures, and took a bus to Augusta. Seven months later, you came into my life and I have never regretted one minute of it."

"Weren't his parents willing to help you?"

"No, they as much as said they never wanted to see me or my baby."

I felt a pain in my stomach, "They didn't ever want to see me?" My mother shook her head.

"How about your parents, didn't they want to help you?"

Again, my mother slowly shook her head. "No, they essentially abandoned us."

I began to understand the pain and rejection my mother felt at being scorned by everyone. At that moment, I started to appreciate what my mother had endured. I felt a son's love for her strength and sacrifice to have and take care of me.

"As you know, we have lived on welfare ever since you were born. This is the first time I have a real job and we are through with that system and all its horrors."

"Did Lovejoy ever ask you to do something that you didn't want to do?"

At that point, my mother's face hardened. Her tears stopped and she said, "He asked many times, and he got nothing but trouble. I took care of that."

At that moment, I understood what a strong, determined, and a decent woman my mother was.

"Do I have any aunts or uncles?" I naively asked.

"Neither Bob nor I have any siblings, so no."

So, my mother had never been married. She had given me her last name. Her parents had disowned her and she was forced to live in the town where I was born. She said I was a mistake, but it didn't matter to her.

She loved me; she had given up everything for me. I told her that I loved her, and that I was proud of the Connor name. I would honor it for the rest of my life. I also made a promise to her that I would always be there for her, to protect her, to avenge any more disrespect done to her. It was a promise I would keep.

"Thank you, Robbie, you make me proud."

Silently though, I swore to square the debt to Lovejoy. I would make him miserable.

"What about Roy, Mom? Wasn't he the right kind of man for us?"

"Robbie, Roy was just the sort of man I would have married. He asked me several times, but marrying him would have meant staying in Augusta with all the baggage of our lives, so I told him, no."

"But, Roy could..."

"I wanted to be free of the gossip and innuendo. There were enough untrue stories about Roy and me as it was."

"But Roy loves you, Mom. He would be a good..."

"Possibly, Robbie, possibly. However, I couldn't take people talking behind our backs calling me all sorts of vile things. No, we needed to be done with that."

"But Roy would have made a good father for me," I whined.

"He would have, probably. He may have been a good husband to me, but I must be on my own. I have to prove that I can live my life without someone making decisions for me or 'caring' for me."

"But, Mom, I wish…"

"There is something else that I have been wanting to say to you, Robbie. You are growing up quickly and I have been too timid to bring up the subject. I have asked Roy if he would talk to you about manly things. Has he?"

"I don't think so, Mom. What manly things?"

"Robbie, this is not easy for me. You are reaching the age where you are starting to get interested in girls. I am asking you to respect any girls you eventually date. It is very important to me. Just keep in mind what I have said today and do talk to Roy."

It was becoming clear to me that she knew more about my secrets than I realized. Those deep dreams and what resulted, which always woke me up. Of course, she knows, Stupid, she knows all about you.

"Okay, Mom, I will talk to Roy when I go to the farm in June."

"Thank you, Robbie, it will ease my mind. Thank you for understanding me."

"Of course, Mom."

I knew Mom was embarrassed to explain about sex to a growing teenage son. After her frank admission to me about the "visits" of the old man Lovejoy, she couldn't bring herself to explain any more about that. In her mind, Roy seemed to be the best option for a kid to help me understand what was happening to my body.

I do admit that at this age, things were still not all that clear to me but I knew that she would call Roy and ask him to explain "things" to me when I went back to Augusta to work. However, didn't she know that a person can't live next to a farm and not have some idea of what's going on in that world even if my immature ideas about it were wrong.

Mom had insisted that I not work with Roy the summer before my freshman year of high school, so I spent a long boring summer in Bards Crossing. She felt I should enjoy my boyhood. What she meant by that, she never explained, but now, I believe that she was feeling the first effects of the "empty nest."

I did know that I missed working with my friend Roy. The summer dragged by without any accomplishments for me. Mom admitted that she may have made a mistake by not allowing me to work in Augusta.

I have much more to say about Bards Crossing, but that story must wait a bit. I promised to relate to you about my experiences that I had on Roy's farm during my high school summers.

Chapter Four

On June third, my first high school year at Alice Day was done. Mom had purchased a bus ticket for me to make the hundred-mile trip back to Augusta. My excitement was very high because I would be on my way to Augusta for my summer job at Roy's farm, and in July, I would be turning fifteen. I was thrilled.

On that day I left Bards Crossing, I enjoyed the feeling of freedom for the first time in my brief life. Being away from Mom for the summer was so grown-up, but I knew it was an illusion. It still felt good even though I knew my freedom was only for the summer.

I knew I would want to get back to Mom and yes, school. She would be lonely, I thought. Also, I would want to share my summer events with my new classmates at Alice Day.

The bus ride was longer than I envisioned. Several stops to pick up and let riders off along the route greatly expanded the travel time and discomfort. First, I had to sit on a scratchy, partially torn seat cushion because all the good seats were already taken. And worse yet, I had to sit next to a man who didn't know the first thing about hygiene. I wanted to move but for the entire first half of the trip, every seat remained filled even with riders coming and going.

After what seemed like the millionth stop, the man got off the bus and was replaced by a girl about my age. I would have taken the stinky man's seat but it was just as dilapidated as mine. I tried to talk with her but she only replied in clipped answers. There was no connection, so I gave up. We were both too shy, I guess.

When the bus finally arrived at the station, Roy was waiting to pick me up. Sitting alongside him was one of the prettiest women I had seen.

"Roy," I thought, "you are a chick magnet."

Her name was Heidi Grant. She had a sweet voice, which was complemented by a small, sensuous mouth. Her big blue eyes looked directly at me when Roy introduced us. She had a very beautiful, unblemished face with a small nose and long eyelashes. She had blond hair, which I believed, at my tender age, was her real hair color. She had a slender, curvaceous body as far as I could see. It wasn't until she got out of the car to greet me that I could see she stood about five-foot five. Her dress was closely fitted around her body revealing a well-developed bosom.

That I had offensive thoughts I am willing to admit. However, I was embarrassed knowing that she was with Roy, and Roy was kind to me. It felt like I was double-crossing him. But these were things that a developing teenaged boy was overpowered by.

When she extended her hand to shake mine, I felt awkward and gangly. I was much taller that she was, but I hadn't yet filled out. I stood there not knowing what to say until Roy said that she wouldn't bite. What she thought of me that day I wasn't sure, but I know what I was thinking about her. I hoped that she and Roy would overlook my apparent timidity and not think I was stupid.

I had no idea of her age, but Roy told me later that she was twenty-five. At my age, anyone who was beyond high school years, was old. Mom was in her early thirties and I believed that she was old. As it turned out, Heidi would eventually convince me that anyone in their mid-twenties was not old.

I learned that Roy had called Mom and told her he had someone living with him, but there was plenty of room for me. What Mom thought of that situation, she never revealed to me. I suspect that she was not particularly pleased about it. I thought it was great.

The ride to the farm was not dull with Roy talking a mile a minute and Heidi chipping in whenever Roy made one of his jokes. The conversation and the scent of Heidi's perfume put me in a mode of thinking that wasn't proper, but for a boy entering manhood, it couldn't be helped. She was beautiful to me.

When we reached the farm, I could see that things had changed for the better. The big house had been painted a soft yellow to hide the garish green color of forty years. The window shutters were now a shiny black and had obviously been repaired by someone with carpentry skills.

The barn had been painted to complement the house color and the dusty, gravel driveway had been paved. More important, in a way, the interior of the barn had received a coat of whitewash to sanitize it.

When I asked Roy about the changes, he replied that he had recently purchased the entire farm, house, and acreage from old man Hubbard's estate after his death two months before. Roy didn't say it outright, but he implied that he had come into a large inheritance, which permitted him to buy and fix-up the old farm.

Until that point, I had thought Roy owned the farm. I had no idea that that he only rented it. I realized how tense and fragile he must have been trying to keep it all together. He had never allowed the strain to surface and affect his usual calm demeanor. I had new respect for Roy.

Two new, shiny John Deere tractors had now replaced the tired Allis-Chalmers, which had been the work horses of the farm for many years. These tractors were the biggest Deere made and I couldn't wait to have Roy let me drive them.

When Roy took me into the barn, I could see he had made many more changes. The milking machines and refrigerators were all new. The old task of lugging milk pails to the refrigerators was replaced by pumps which now forced the milk to flow directly into the new style refrigerated holding tanks. Moreover, Roy had more than doubled the size of his herd.

"Untouched by human hands," Roy said, with pride and a bit of bravado, which I believed he had the right to do.

I felt good for Roy and his farm. Money had provided the equipment that made operation of a dairy farm possible. I knew that I would love working with Roy this summer.

Roy had also purchased a couple of new dump-body trucks. One was kept at the farm, and the other was parked at the big saw mill to collect sawdust. When it was full, Roy would drive the spare one to the mill to replace the loaded truck.

"Roy, why do you keep using the sawdust bedding?"

"Some people think it isn't the best, but it is the most comfortable for my cows and I want happy cows." That was typically Roy; keep "his babies" happy.

The old method of sawdust bedding for the cows was something that Roy said he would always keep doing. I saw his logic and the cows did seem happy being cows.

Roy told me that he would pay me one hundred dollars a week, but that seventy-five had to be sent to Mom for safekeeping. Apparently, she and Roy had made this agreement. At first, I protested to Mom, but she insisted that this money was for college, so I quit my whining.

Roy also told me that the farm work was only part of the duties I would have. I was expected to help with the laundry once a week and to help with meals by setting the table and such. I thought that Heidi would be taking care of the meals and laundry. It was another opportunity for me to learn something.

When we started work the next day, Heidi pitched in with the farm chores dressed in her farmer's overalls and short sleeved top. Now it made sense to me. She was a farm girl fully prepared to help me and Roy and me with the farm chores. Roy and I were expected to help with the domestic side of living. It was only fair.

One day I made the mistake of calling her overalls

dungarees. Why she was offended by that I never learned. After seeing how she reacted, I didn't make that mistake again.

Remembering things about my nightly dreams, I didn't want Heidi to wash my clothes. It would be too embarrassing for me. So, I volunteered to do all the washing on Sunday. Both Roy and Heidi said that was not necessary but I insisted.

I believe at the time there may have been some prurient reasons for my insistence about the laundry. As usual, I was not smart enough to realize that she and Roy could figure that one out. I discovered that Heidi's under things were never in the hampers.

As the summer progressed, I began to admire, yes, even love Heidi. She stood by Roy helping him to do the most menial chores with never a complaint. She could handle tractors and trucks much better than I could, and she was always willing to teach me when I ran into trouble. She was petite. Nevertheless, she did a man's work as well as any man, except for Roy.

Heidi was more than Roy's partner and I should have respected that immediately. But as a thoughtless teenager, anyone was fair game; hormones ruled the day and night, much to my chagrin sometimes.

By the end of the summer, I was embarrassed for my early thoughts. My lustful thoughts had morphed into admiration and yes, real love for Roy's partner. My teenage mind could admit love without embarrassment.

Notwithstanding my inexperience with the mysteries of life, I meant it in the same way I made the silent vow as I had for Mom. I would protect them both with all my energy, or so I thought.

Roy and Mom must have communicated over the summer because he took time to explain "things" to me and give his advice in how to handle the opposite sex. It might as well have been Mom talking to me. "Respect the girls you go out with. Don't do anything that you will regret." Roy wasn't a prude, but he had moral standards. I respected Roy's advice but I wasn't sure I could follow it back at Bards Crossing. Time would tell.

Roy also talked to me about a topic I had never really considered in my youthful mind.

"Robbie, do you know what a friend is?" Roy asked one day.

"Yeah, a friend is like my friend Abner in Bards Crossing," I answered wondering what Roy was asking.

"What makes him a friend, Robbie?" Roy pushed.

"I don't know what you mean, Roy."

"Well, is he someone you can tell things to and know he will not blab them to others?"

"Yeah, he is. We talk about a lot of things and I know he keeps it to himself."

"Do you keep those things to yourself, Robbie?"

"Yeah, when we swear not to tell someone else, I do."

"So, you trust each other, right?"

"Yeah, I do. He is my friend."

"Friendship is a complicated thing, Robbie. Being a friend means that you are dependable and are trusted by another person. It means, in many ways, that you would trust them with your life, if necessary.

"If you were married, you would trust them with your wife to be there for her if you could not, and to not violate or hurt her. You would trust them with your worldly possessions.

"A friend is someone you can trust under any circumstances, Robbie. In life, a person is very, very lucky if he or she has one or two friends. The rest of people we know and interact with and call 'friends' are really 'acquaintances,' not true friends. Understand?"

"Yes, Roy, but…"

"So, is Abner really your friend?"

"He is, Roy and I think we are friends."

"How many friends do you think you have?"

"I think Abner is a very close friend."

"I think there are three more, Robbie. One is your mom and the other is Heidi. They both love you and would never betray you. I want you to know that, to me, you are a friend, a good friend, a real friend. Think that over."

"Who are your friends?" I asked.

"Well, Heidi is first and foremost my best friend, then your Mom, John is very special to me, you, of course, as I have said. Other than that, the rest of the people I know are acquaintances."

"Is John the old man Janek?"

"He is."

"What about family, Roy? Aren't they real friends?"

"Family members may or may not be friends. Anyway, you can't do anything about family. Some you like, some you don't."

With that, the conversation ended, but the things Roy said to me occupied my thinking for many years. He was right about many things in life. He was right about our friendship. I felt the same about him.

Chapter Five

That summer, I spent many evening hours thinking about the life lessons Roy shared with me. His beliefs about friendship and his sense of justice became a part of my psyche.

Perhaps more important, I learned about farming. My mind was learning the business, practical, social, and a human side of dealing with people and the rigor of tending to animals and crops. My muscles were discovering the effort it takes to keep a farm active and vibrant. Roy taught me that "farming" is a way of life, not a job.

In addition to the other daily routines to tend the animals, which I have already described, several times that summer we cut field grass, then raked, tedded, dried and baled the winter feed. We loaded the bales onto trucks and hauled them to the barn where we team lugged the bales up into the hay loft. The chore was sweaty, dusty, and caused itching, which to this day, I can still feel on the back of my neck and arms. The long, hot showers taken those nights were so welcome to restore my mind and body. Sleep came quickly along with my crazy, sensual dreams.

On the fourth of July, my birthday, the idyllic aura of this summer was badly shaken. A murder occurred on Roy's farm. The murder victim was Janek Gulden; the old man who worked with Roy and had helped me at milking time. The man had been beaten and his throat slit by some unknown, heartless trash. As I recounted to you earlier, he had lived for many years on the farm in the small house located beside the pasture road.

Before Roy took over the farm, Janek had worked for the previous farmer. He was fifteen years old at the time. His work agreement was to receive a small weekly sum and allowed to live in the small pasture road house. The farmer did not require any rent.

The tiny house had a combination living, kitchen, and dining area. A door led to a tiny bedroom having a bed, a chair and a bedside table and lamp. Sometime in the life of this house, it had been electrified so at least Janek some semblance of a home. The house had running water, but no interior bathroom. A sink which at times would not drain, a noisy refrigerator and a cranky gas range to cook his meals completed the kitchen.

After Roy purchased the farm, he made many upgrades to the farm, its buildings, and Janek's house, which Roy revamped entirely. Roy installed new kitchen appliances and added a proper bathroom. He told Janek that he could live there as long as he wanted. He also improved the building to make Janek's bedroom larger.

Once, Roy had said to me, "No man should have to live that way." Roy had a heart.

Janek's death pushed me to reminisce about the first year I went to the barn after school to help Janek and Roy with the chores. By that time, Janek was somewhat fat and his dungaree overalls were stretched to their limit. He had a gray beard and his hair was always unkempt, but clean. He had some trouble doing the chores because of his advanced age and weight, but he was always kind to me by doing the work my small muscles couldn't do.

Janek spoke with a strong accent. Roy told me he thought Janek was Dutch. He called himself Janek and he called me Jedrek which I thought was cool. I didn't really know about Janek's life except what Heidi would later tell me.

When Roy had offered me an after-school job, Janek limited his helping to the milking routine, twice daily. I would see Janek occasionally in the barn at other times talking to Roy.

Janek was not always treated kindly by Augusta residents. Occasionally at night, a few roughneck neighborhood kids would throw stones at Janek's house and taunt the old man. Roy would go out and fire his shotgun into the air to scare them off, but that wasn't always enough. Often, they would return. Roy reported the incidents to the Augusta police. They were never able to nab the culprits.

On this horrendous day, Roy had gone to check on Janek as he did every day before starting chores. He usually brought him a cup of coffee and they would chat for a few minutes. That morning was horrible. Roy discovered the gore and vomited.

The police arrived shortly after Heidi called.

After looking at the dreadful scene, the detective began to ask Roy a question, but Heidi intervened.

"Can't you see this man is distraught? I'll answer your

questions."

"Thank you, Heidi," Roy said, "I'll be all right. What's your question, Detective?"

"Do you know the victim?"

"I do, he lives her and helps me on the farm."

"What is his name?"

"You must be new around here, Detective, everyone knows him as John Goldie, but that isn't his real name; it's just what people call him. His name is Janek Gulden.

"He's been on this farm long before I took it over. One time I asked him where he had come from. He said that he was from the Netherlands. Other than that, I have no idea."

"When was the last time you saw him?"

"It was around eight-thirty last evening. We had a cup of coffee and after I went home."

"Do you have any idea who might have done this?"

"No."

"I checked the call records to this house. Were any of the troublemakers here last night?"

"Not that I know. It was quiet last night, so I don't believe they were. When they do come around, I can hear them from my bedroom."

"Do you know if he had any other usual visitors at night?"

"If you mean family members, I can tell you he had none. He was alone in this world. He told me that one time. I asked what he meant. All he said was, 'It was a long time ago. They're all gone.' "

"What was his daily routine?"

"He usually helped me with the milking. He had a little vegetable garden. He would tend that and sit on the back porch smoking a cigar. We often saw him walking along the pasture road. He would go to Flynn's Package store and pick up beer. He didn't have a driver's license and he told me that he received very little from social security.

"He has worked for me for as long as I have had the farm. When he was working, I paid him a hundred dollars a month with free housing, which wasn't much at the time. Recently, he and I agreed that many of the chores of the farm were too much for him; he would do what he could, which was fine with me.

"I paid him a small amount each a week so he would have some spending money. He had been such a loyal and good worker for the previous farmer and me that it just seemed right.

"On Saturday mornings, he would tell Heidi what groceries he needed for the week. She would pick them up. John always offered to pay but we never accepted his offer."

"So as far as you know, he had no regular visitors?"

"No."

"Do you know if he had any money stashed here? The bedroom has been ransacked. We haven't found any valuables or cash."

"I really have no idea. John didn't talk about things like that. He probably accumulated money over the years, but I honestly don't know. Other than his beer and cigars, I don't know what he spent money on."

"Okay, Roy, we have to seal off the house. The forensics folks need to be here for the next day or so. Even after that it will be off-limits until we say you can open it."

"I understand. We don't need it, anyway."

Years later, it was still unoccupied.

It was obvious that Roy was extremely impacted by his friend's murder. Funeral arrangements needed to be made, but Roy didn't seem to have the strength to make the decisions. Heidi took charge and handled all that needed to be done. The funeral was held as soon as the official procedures were complete.

That day, I saw a side of Roy I had never seen even on the day of the murder. His usual quiet demeanor gave way to tears sliding down his cheeks. His body shook in a way that made me believe he would not make it through the funeral. He leaned against Heidi to keep from falling. It was then I appreciated the strength of Heidi and realized the power of the bond that held them together.

I had called Mom about the killing. Her first response was that I should come home immediately. I didn't want that. I asked Roy to talk to her. He calmed Mom down enough for her to agree to let me finish the summer with them.

The rest of July dragged by. The murder had taken a dreadful toll on all our emotions. We knew that a vicious murderer had not been captured. That bothered us so much that our sleep was disturbed many times during the night.

Often, I could hear Heidi and Roy quietly talking. I would not have been surprised if they were planning to sell out. For selfish reasons, I hoped they wouldn't. I was still enjoying farm life, freedom from Mom, and the feeling I was accomplishing something.

I knew that I would have to work on Mom to let me return next summer. But I was coming back, no matter what.

Finally, around the first of August we received good news. The police had apprehended a drifter who had a long police record and was in the area the night of the murder.

Supplied with an attorney, he had his hearing in court and he was bound over for the Grand Jury's decision. The surprise came a week later when the Grand Jury refused to submit a True Bill. The police had no choice but to release him. They had no indictable evidence.

When the police told us that the drifter was out of jail, I said to Roy showing my judicial ignorance, "Why would they let a killer go?"

"Because some lowlife lawyer let him escape."

I chuckled to myself because Roy always said some words like a New Yorker: 'excape' not escape, 'axe me', not ask me!

The police told the drifter to move on, but he refused to leave Augusta. Somehow, he had enough money to rent a motel room and get himself a new set of clothes. The clothes were not fancy, but it seemed they were more than a bum could afford.

Two days after his release, he was found clubbed to death behind the supermarket building on Prince Street. He had been brutally beaten with a baseball bat. The police knew what the murder weapon was because the killer had left it for them. It had no fingerprints on it. For the police, it was another dead end.

The police questioned many people in the city. Their efforts produced no suspects and the cases of John Goldie and the unknown killer of the drifter went cold. Roy felt that they would never be solved. Heidi thought it would be solved. She had faith in the police.

"Why do you think they will never be solved?" I asked.

"Robbie, don't ever forget the old saying: 'What goes around; is what comes around,' " and then he just smiled that familiar smile. What did he know? He certainly talked to many people. Perhaps they had influenced his thinking. I felt that way also, but I didn't know why. But I'll say more about that later.

When I had "worked" for Roy at the time we lived in Augusta, he and I would go into the silo and bag up the ensilage for feed to augment the hay. This was supplemental feed for the cows in the winter. Since I only worked after school, I had never been part of filling the silo. That summer, though, I would learn much more about the value of silos to dairy farming including the growing of "cow corn" on Roy's rented fields and the equipment needed to fill those silos.

In late August, we began to harvest corn for ensilage. It took the three of us; Roy drove the huge ensilage harvester which cut, or rather diced the corn stalks and then blew them into a truck driving alongside the boom. As you can guess, Heidi and I were the truck drivers.

When a truck was full, the second truck would immediately pull up to replace it as the first one left the field for the silo. The system was so smooth that it was not necessary to stop the harvester. What little ensilage was sprayed onto the ground during the substitution was minimal.

Roy had already trained me for my first trip to the silo. Using the dump-body feature of the truck, I would slowly allow the ensilage to slide into a hopper connected to a huge blower driving the silage into the top of the silo where it accumulated. When I had emptied my truck, I returned to the field and "seconded" the truck Heidi was driving. She would then drive to the silo and empty her truck. This daily process would continue until it was nearly milking time and then resume the next day when the morning milking was done. By the time the total corn harvesting was finished, the ensilage would reach the top of the silo just below the roof. It would be enough to provide feed through the winter months.

The end of August came quickly and I made plans to return home. The corn harvesting was not finished, but Roy said a farmer from a neighboring town would help them complete the task.

And so I boarded the bus back to Bards Crossing. I knew this would be my last bus trip because next summer I would be driving a car to Augusta. How I would get that car, I didn't know, but I was sure it would happen. I just needed to work on Mom about it.

The next two summers seemed to fly by. The last summer I worked for Roy was between my high school graduation and start of college. After all the good times with Roy, Heidi, and the farm, and as much as I loved farming, I knew that my future career lay beyond the constant responsibility of running a dairy farm. For a youngster growing up, the experience was exciting and wholesome, but as an adult it offered long hours, heavy labor, massive vet bills, small profit, and no assurance of success. I knew it was not for me.

Several days before I was due to leave, Heidi requested that I go with her to pick up a load of sawdust from the sawmill. On the way to the lumber mill, Heidi opened a discussion I did not expect.

"Robbie, remember when John died two summers ago?"

"How could I forget that? It was a terrible thing."

"I know that you were very surprised to see how Roy reacted because of John's death."

She and Roy always referred to Janek using his English Christian name, John

"I was surprised, Heidi," I stammered, not quite knowing what else to say, "Roy is always so strong."

"I am going to tell you something that you must not ever

47

mention to anyone, not even your mother."

"I don't understand, Heidi," I said while she pulled the truck to the side of the road, "Why? Is it such a secret?"

"There are things Roy has told me, and there are things I have discovered about Roy. He and I share matters that are only meant to be known between husbands and wives."

"Heidi, should you be talking to me about Roy this way?" I asked.

"Yes, Robbie, you need to know some things. John was more to Roy than some work hand too old to handle the chores. He was more, much more to Roy.

"What I am going to say happened many years ago, but Roy only found out about the time when you and your mum moved away to Bards Crossing."

"Mom said…"

"You know that your mother and Roy became very close for a while, but that is not what I want to say. I'm worldlier that your mum, so when you folks left, I came along and filled a need in Roy's life that your mum could not.

"I was what he needed and still needs. Let me continue. Around that time, Roy received a letter from his Aunt Aretha. The letter said that Roy should know that his farm hand's real name was Janek Gulden, who had come to this country from the Netherlands. Since he spoke very broken English, people called him John Goldie.

"She said that rumor had it that John was wanted in his homeland for some crime he committed, but she did not elaborate. The letter contained many facts that Roy could verify, so he knew that what his aunt was writing was the truth. She had written the letter a few years before her death with instructions to send it to Roy after she died."

"But what did the letter have to do with Goldie and Roy?" I stupidly asked.

"I'm getting to that; be patient, Robbie. Roy grew up without a father, like you. His mother, Linda, was married to James Hepburn for a couple of years. James died in a car crash before Roy was born, but at the time of James death, Linda was not pregnant. Sometime, shortly after James' death, John, Janek, made his appearance in the town where Linda was living. The letter said that John and Linda became friendly, too friendly because she got pregnant. The relationship with John didn't last; she moved on with her life.

"She only had one child, Robbie, and that was Roy. Roy's birth certificate listed James Hepburn as the father. No one was the wiser, since she moved to Augusta before Roy was born. She never told him the truth. She died of cancer. It was the same year he turned eighteen.

"After high school, Roy went into the Army for two years. After that, he bummed around for a few years until he got control of himself and had the opportunity to buy the farm in Augusta. As fate would have it, John had worked as a hand on the farm for years and had stayed on after the purchase. As you know, he lived in the little house next to the pasture road.

"It was only after Roy received the letter that he had any

inkling about his real paternity. At first, he raged about having been lied to by his mother. I was able to calm him down and make him realize how embarrassing it must have been to put herself in that position. After some time, Roy finally accepted that his mother sacrificed much to protect and love him. The lie was unimportant.

"Roy finally got up the nerve to confront John; not in an angry or hostile way, but to learn as much as he could about his 'real' father. John confirmed much of the letter's information. The impact on Roy was hard to define. On one hand, he felt John was a cad for not marrying his mum; on the other, he was grateful he now knew his father's identity.

"After that, Roy spent many hours with him. Before Roy's mum died, she had confessed to her sister, Aretha, naming John as Roy's father. Obviously, it had remained a secret to Roy until the letter arrived.

"As you know, Robbie, Roy is very intense about things that happen to people that he loves. After John's murder, he was not himself until the suspect in John's death was himself killed. Roy has told me that if bad things happen to people he loves, he can't rest until justice has been done. I have asked him what he means by that, but he just smiles.

"Robbie, there is another thing I would like to say. I feel it is important now as you leave us. There is a reason that Roy has treated you in a special way. His first wife, as you know, was killed in a hunting accident. What Roy doesn't talk about is that she was pregnant when she was killed.

"When I came along, it became apparent that we could

not have children. That stopped any possibility of him ever having children because he would never leave me. Roy considers you his son, but you know that Roy could never crack his shell to say it. He is your friend and your father in every way that he can. If he and your mum had married, he would have adopted you. He loves you, Robbie, never forget that."

"You must never tell Roy what I have told you today. In many ways he is a proud but private man, but I felt that you should know."

"Roy told me one time what it meant to be a friend to someone. He said, 'A true friend is a person you can share fantasies or fears and that person would never reveal the privacy of what's been said.' I don't know what to think about what you've told me," I questioned.

"Just be aware of what I've said, Robbie. I would never betray Roy because he is my best friend. You needed to know," Heidi said firmly.

As the waning days of that last summer finally forced my packing to leave, we said our final good-byes. Heidi and Roy both had tears in their eyes. I can tell you that mine were not dry either and I was not ashamed. Heidi had been a surrogate mother for me on the farm and Roy, without question, was my real father.

My emotions finally wouldn't allow me to leave without saying to Roy that I loved him. Stoic Roy mumbled something that I knew was his way of saying that he loved me also. I hugged him. I told Heidi I loved her.

I told them that I would come back whenever I could to visit them and the farm. We agreed to write whenever possible, but we promised each other to phone once a month. I would phone them or they would call me.

It turned out that the writing commitment was sketchy, and even the phone calls happened frequently for a while. Life's pressures, however, altered even that. As the years went by the calls became infrequent; we understood why; life was moving on for all of us. But we were friends and would be for life.

A few years later, Roy and Heidi invited me to visit them, but I could not at that time. The pain of that missed opportunity has remained with me to this day. As it turned out, I only saw Roy's farm one more time and that was a depressing day.

Chapter Six

As promised, I must continue the story of my life with Mom. I need to tell you more about Bards Crossing where I grew into manhood and flew off into independent life, well, almost. Mom still had to guide me through the college years.

Bards Crossing was where I met Abner Smith. He and Roy were the two best male friends I had in my life. We met in the Freshman General Science class at Alice Day Regional High School. As I had with Roy, we connected immediately, sharing similar ideas and interests.

Abner had black hair which he wore longer than Mom allowed me to keep mine. He had a pleasant face, dark brown eyes and a nose that fit nicely, not too large or small. Unlike mine, his ears were acceptably close to his head with unlocked lobes.

Abner had an intimidating bearing. He was nearly six feet tall with a full chest and strong arms to match. It was clear at this age, he could have grown a beard had he wished.

In general, he had a friendly disposition. His behavior toward me and other classmates was calm, but there were a few incidents when he displayed a strong temper, never toward me, I must admit.

Abner, unlike me, had two parents. One time he told me that he always felt as though he had been a mistake in their lives, and they had some resentment for his intrusion. His mother would occasionally invite me over for after-school snacks. Abner's family seemed close knit and I felt warmth in their invitations. Abner's mother said he was more than twelve pounds when he was born and grew up too fast, whatever that meant. It didn't seem to me that his parents resented Abner's birth as he thought it had.

Another thing about Abner was that he was smart, very smart. There was no question that our teachers could ask which he didn't know the answer. It was another feature of him that drew me as a friend to him. My mother thought that Abner was the perfect friend for me. He was always invited to our home for dinner and to work our homework sessions when needed.

Abner Smith had been named Abner Beverly Smith by his parents who apparently didn't appreciate the impact on a young man growing up in a world where the petty viciousness of children could inflict pain for something simple as a name. In Abner's mind, his parents might as well have named him Mary or Fanny; the result would be the same. He tried very hard to keep the middle name secret. Someone always found it out. The girl-sounding name encouraged would-be pranksters.

Woe would be to them that tried it, though. Many, who taunted with a sing-song voice, left the school with bloody noses or blackened eyes.

Since I was always with Abner, we both got to "see" the principal and explain our behavior. We were assigned more than our fair share of in-school suspensions.

There have always been bullies and Bards Crossing had

its share when Mom and I relocated there. Even though I was almost as tall as Abner, I didn't have his physique, or worse, his character to stand up for myself. He decided that I needed his help.

When it came to fights, I was the "ninety-pound weakling," but that eventually changed under Abner's fitness program. He introduced me to body building and it was not long before I could hold my own in any situation.

It was clear from the start that Abner and I were not popular with our classmates. He and I shared similar traits and interests; one was that we both were interested in science; real science, not fake science.

That first year, we worked on a science fair project; studied together and were content with each other's company. Some people think that is bad, but that established a bond between us. We ate our lunches alone and usually walked home discussing things which interested us. We spent time at each other's homes although his mother was not quite as receptive as mine to our spontaneous invitations to dinner.

When I think about our years at Alice Day, it seems to me that some of our classmates didn't dislike us as much as they feared us. True, we defended ourselves, but we didn't bully them.

Events changed for us in our sophomore year. We tried out for the football team and were quickly selected. We soon we realized what a good decision we had made. We became big men on campus, but it also meant long practice hours and pain.

We were big, strong and Coach Fox needed us. He wanted a winning team that season and we were his picks for the center (Abner) and (me) tackle.

For Coach Fox, his dream of a winning team became a reality that year. Abner and I were solid linemen. He had chosen several backs and an outstanding quarterback who would eventually play for Alabama and the NFL. Our seasons were 7-0, 7-0, and 6-1.

Our senior year, we lost the last game. Two weeks before our final game, our best running back, Jerry Billings and best receiver, Joe March, were killed in a car accident. The police said that they had tried to outrun a freight train.

When something like this happens, you realize how tight teams are. It demoralizes a team. Our sadness remained with us in the final game. We just couldn't play with determination and heart.

The other major change in our lives was the discovery that as football men, we had our pick of the prettiest girls. It meant girls, girls, girls. I have already told you about the hormone drive, especially mine, during those years.

Abner was no different and we often double-dated with junior and senior classmates. I must confess that I didn't always obey Mom's dictum to "Respect the girls you are dating." In fact, as you might imagine, we often dated the ones with the easiest reputations. Oh, the memories.

Even so, it was in our senior years, that Abner and I found love, real love. I began going steady with Anne Fox, yes, she was the coach's daughter.

Anne, in my eyes was the best-looking girl of the entire high school. Standing at five-foot six, she had beautiful blond hair, stunning blue eyes and a very pretty face with a petite nose and warm smile. Her figure made my heart skip a few beats. Anne reminded me of Heidi in many ways. She had a calm and agreeable disposition that attracted many to her.

Before she dated me, she had dated guys in the class, including some on the football team. Because she was the coach's daughter, most didn't try anything with her. That didn't stop me, but she had strong morals that stopped me from being a fool. She was a virgin when we finally wed.

Abner started dating Maryanne Evans, who in my mind was nothing special to look at, except that her figure made men notice. Abner told me he was a boob man, so she fit the bill. It was clear that she loved Abner from the start. Anyone that loved Abner was okay in my book.

Maryanne was pretty in a plain sort of way with long brown hair, an unexceptional face, and a smile what wasn't always warm when directed at me. In fact, her personality tended to be rather waspish at the expected times. It seemed to me to be a small character flaw, but that view would be revisited given what happened much later. She would sometimes correct Abner in public using a tone of voice I wouldn't have accepted. Abner loved her.

Abner told me that she was like Anne in that she didn't fool around before marriage. So, I guess that she was also a virgin when they finally married.

Abner and Maryanne went to the state university in Colorado, while Anne attended a small college in New York. I stayed closer to home and attended the up-state university.

Quite coincidentally, Abner and I majored in the field of criminal justice. We had talked many different times about careers in high school, so it was not a surprise when we realized that we had made the same career choice. As for the women, Maryanne majored in early childhood education and Anne received her degree in social studies.

My career plan was to find a position in a small police force and work my way up the ladder. Abner decided to go on to law school. His goal was to join the FBI and capture the really bad guys.

Abner married Maryanne and I wed Anne. We, the men, had hoped to have a double wedding ceremony. Since that topic hadn't been discussed with the two women, we decided to abandon that idea. In fact, the problem was that the two women each wanted their own day, not a shared one. Being men, we had not considered that.

It had not occurred to Abner and me that our "loves" did not really like each other. They played the game until marriage. I'll give them credit for that.

Abner and Maryanne wed first. We attended and I was Abner's best man. Anne was not Maryanne's bridesmaid. Anne insisted we return the favor when she and I were married two years later. I, of course, asked Abner to be my best man, and Anne had selected her sister, Grace, as her bridesmaid. One important highlight of our wedding was that Roy and Heidi were able to break away from the farm and attend. I could not have been happier to see them.

After the weddings, the years passed rapidly and before the Connors and Smiths realized it, more than ten years had elapsed since we had last spoken. Our communications over those years had been birthday and holiday cards with the perfunctory "love you, let's get together soon" notes before scrawled signatures. The long-distance friendship had endured. Abner and I remained friends, but were seldom able to meet.

However, a chance meeting at a professional seminar regenerated the friendship Abner and I had known in high school. We enjoyed a couple of drinks that evening. It was enjoyable covering the highlights of our high school years.

We shared some information about our marriages and how well family life agreed with us. But it was beginning to look as though neither Abner nor I would be a father anytime soon, if ever.

Abner, after drinking a little too much, began to share an intimate detail about his relationship with Maryanne. It seemed he was going to talk about private things that I felt I should not hear. I could gather enough of the problems before I stopped him from saying too much. I didn't tell Abner that my marriage was warm and I loved Anne a bit more each day. As a friend I couldn't hurt him, but I had always felt that Maryanne was not the best match for him.

After law school, Abner had applied for and accepted a position with the FBI. My position, at the time, was the local police chief of a small city called Alton miles away from Augusta. It had taken me several years to pin on the Chief's tin. It was here that I led a police force of five officers and two detectives. Not necessarily impressive, but it allowed me to buy a small, warm home for Anne and me. We were happy and Anne's work at the local college was rewarding for her.

Abner's career path gave me a twinge of remorse and made me reconsider my career status. He encouraged me to think about moving to a larger city where I could make myself more valuable in the criminal justice world.

At the end of the seminar, Abner and I agreed to meet again sometime soon; re-introduce our wives; party and reminisce over the great times we had together.

The next day, I put my plans into action and filled out applications. I would not achieve my goal for a few more years. Serendipitously, life would bring Abner and me together again.

Chapter Seven

It was a Thursday that I would never forget. A call came into my office phone. People calling the Alton Police Department were routed to the routine business line. I knew this call was unusual. The only people who had my direct line were Anne, Mom, Roy, and Heidi.

Roy's ID came up. It was strange for Roy or Heidi to call me at this time of day and to call on my office phone. They always called me in the evening on my cell phone.

At first, I could not understand what Roy was saying.

"Roy, what is the matter?" I nearly yelled.

There was only more of the same incoherence.

"Roy, please, put Heidi on the phone," I demanded.

With that, Roy settled down enough to give me the reason he called.

"Robbie, Heidi has died."

"What? What happened, Roy? Was she sick?"

"No, Robbie, some sick son-of-a-bitch killed her. She went to visit her father in Portland and also to have dinner with a college friend."

"Oh no, Roy," I moaned, as a sick feeling in my stomach began, nearly forcing me to think I was going to vomit. "Anne and I will be there as soon as possible. I am so sorry, Roy. I wish there was something I could do."

"There's nothing much you can do right now, Robbie."

"I know, but we can be there to help in any way we are able to."

"Robbie, if you can come down in a couple of days that

would help."

"Roy, I can't express how much I loved Heidi. She was a mother to me as much as my Mom. I hate this."

"I know, Robbie, she loved you."

"Roy, are you going to be okay?"

"Heidi was my life, Robbie. She was my friend. She knew all my failings and still loved me."

"I know, Roy, she loved you."

"It will be tough getting over this."

"I know, Roy, but the farm will keep you busy."

"Heidi was part of this farm. I am not ashamed to say that I may not have the strength to carry on."

"Please don't talk like that, Roy. You have friends that love you."

"I know, but without Heidi, I have no reason."

"You do! You do! I will come down today."

"No, come in a couple of days. That will help."

"Alright, Roy. I will come down on Saturday."

With that we ended the conversation. I called Anne and Mom at their work with the terrible news.

Of course, their response was disbelief with tears and multiple questions, when, who, what, how? I had no answers.

I needed to learn certain things about Heidi's murder before we left for the farm. So, one of my follow-up calls after Roy's had been to my counterpart at the Portland police department.

"Good morning, Chief Parker, this is Chief Connor from

the Alton police department."

"Good morning, Chief, what can I do for you?"

"You had a murder last night of a Heidi Grant. The reason I am calling is that she was a very special person to me."

"Heidi Grant? Our murder victim is named Heidi Hepburn from the driver's license we found."

"That's odd," I thought to myself, "I had always believed that the wedding bands Roy and Heidi wore were just for show, something to keep tongues from wagging."

"I see. Roy and Heidi must have gotten married. I didn't realize that. I should tell you that both Roy Hepburn and Heidi were very close to me. They were surrogate father and mother when I was growing up," I explained.

"I understand, what is it you want from me?"

"I would like some more information about her murder, if possible."

"Since you are close to both of them, I really can't tell you much. There is a post-mortem being done this morning, so the actual cause of death isn't something I know yet. It's too early to…"

"Roy and Heidi run a dairy farm in Augusta; it is a very time demanding responsibility. As a policeman, I know the husband could be a prime suspect. I just wanted to let you know that they were a very close couple."

"Well, thanks, but the investigation is just beginning, so…"

"I understand, but as your investigation proceeds, I will

bet that you will find he was in Augusta; I would bet my badge on it."

"I really can't comment more, Chief."

"Can you, as a fellow police officer, give me any details of her death?"

"What I can tell you must remain confidential. I will not give you all the details. Some facts have to stay known only to us."

"I promise that I will tell no one, Chief. You have my word."

"Okay, Chief Conner. Ms. Hepburn was found along Canal Street at two a.m. by a patrol car. She had been badly beaten about the head; stabbed several times, apparently; the autopsy will let us know how many; from the looks of her position on the street, she had been displayed.

"She was nearly naked and we believe that she had been raped. Again, the post-mortem will say. It was a brutal crime."

"Do you believe that the murder took place on the street?"

"No, and I don't want this repeated; she was dumped there. The murder took place somewhere else. I don't want to add to your pain about this, but since it wasn't a street murder, she may have been tortured."

"Oh, Christ, Chief."

"Do you know why she was in Portland?"

"Roy had told me that she had gone to see her father. He is in a nursing home and is very ill; near death as far as her

64

husband knows."

For some reason, I didn't share with Chief Parker the fact that Heidi was going to see a friend and go to dinner. I still am not sure why I kept this information from Parker. As he said, he needed to keep some information from me. If this situation were reversed, I would have done the same.

"We'll check on that. Her father's name would be Grant, then?"

"As far as I know, Chief. Thank you, I will keep my word about the details you have given me. I want you to find the savage beast who did this. Thank you again."

With that, I hung up and made preparations to drive my wife and mother to Augusta.

On Saturday, Anne and I left Alton. We picked up Mom in Bards Crossing and drove to Augusta, reaching the farm in the early evening. It was apparent that Roy was in no shape to manage the chores. Two farmers from neighboring towns had volunteered to help, splitting the morning and evening chores to keep the place going.

"Thank you all for coming down," Roy said, greeting us with reddened eyes and husky voice.

"Roy, there is no way we would not have been here," Mom replied.

"Have you had anything to eat today, Roy?" Anne asked.

"No, no appetite."

"Show us to the kitchen," Mom and Anne said in unison. "We'll make a big shepherd's pie for us."

Roy and I sat on the porch. I tried to find out what Roy knew about Heidi's murder. He didn't know much as I supposed he might. As a police chief, I knew that the first suspect is always a family member, so I didn't expect that the Portland police would give him many details of the death.

"Roy, do you know what happened?"

"Other than some son-of-a-bitch killed the love of my life, no."

"Why was she in Portland?"

"She told me that she wanted to see her father. She was going to look up a former friend and catch a dinner."

"Who was the friend?"

"I don't really know, Robbie; she said it was a person who had been special in her life before she met me, a college friend."

"Did that bother you? Seeing a special friend?"

"No, I trusted Heidi. She never lied to me."

"Do you think this special friend could be responsible for her death?"

"Oh, Robbie, I have no idea."

"Well, that is something the Portland police will have to check out."

"Can you tell me anything more about her?"

"What do you mean?"

"Well, was she looking forward to seeing her father? Did they get along?"

"Not really, but he has been in a nursing home for a

couple of years. We had to put him in there. He couldn't take care of himself anymore. She actually owned the house he was living in. She sold it a year ago."

"What happened to her mother?"

"Oh, she died when Heidi was thirteen, so I never met her. Heidi loved her."

"What are you going to do about the farm?"

"Heidi and I had been talking about selling it off and retiring to Glendale. Maybe I'll do that; I don't have the energy to run it alone."

"If there is anything I can do, Roy, please don't hesitate to ask."

"Nah, there is nothing you can do. Thanks."

"Let's go check on the women and see about that shepherd's pie."

After dinner, Roy and I made small talk with Mom and Anne. We stayed with Roy until Monday when we returned home.

A week later, Heidi's body was released for burial. Chief Parker had called me to say for certain that Heidi had been brutalized and raped. It was hard to hear, but I already suspected the grim facts. Those kinds of murder have a certain scenario which plays out. There is violence, degradation of the victim, and finally a horrible death. The only things that change are the perpetrator and victim.

The three of us again returned to Augusta for the burial. It was painful to watch a man's heart ripped from his body. When the interment was over, Roy told us that he would definitely sell the farm and retire.

"Where will you go, Roy?" I asked.

"Heidi and I had been thinking about retirement from the farm. We had already been considering a small cottage on the south shore of Glendale Lake in Glendale. We fell in love with it and decided to buy it. Then some murdering bastard killed her."

On the drive back to Bards Crossing to drop off Mom, I brought up the subject of Roy's marriage to Heidi.

"Mom, when did you know Heidi was coming into Roy's life?"

"Oh, Robbie, it is painful to talk about it."

"I'm sorry. Mom, but I really need to know. I remember talking to you about possibly marrying Roy. You said that wasn't going to happen and then we moved."

"At the time, I really loved Roy and thought we would get married. I wanted to be a farm wife and help Roy any way I could. I had just finished my course work at the college when Roy told me he had met someone. Someone he wanted to be with. I was devastated and decided to move us far away."

"I remember that you were sad and emotional for quite a while before we left. You told me we had to move because you wanted be independent."

"I couldn't bear to tell you why. I felt betrayed for the second time by a man. I swore to myself that I wouldn't allow me to become involved with another man while you were still young. I know what Roy meant to you."

"I'm sorry, Mom."

"Don't be sorry for me, Robbie. I've made another life in Bards Crossing and I don't look back. You got the benefit of growing up in a small town, and you met Anne. That made it all worth it."

"Thank you, Mom," Anne interjected.

"Why did you let me work during the summers with Roy?"

"I'm not small minded, Robbie. I saw the value of Roy's influence on you. I couldn't deprive you of that."

I had always known that my mother wanted the best for me, but I hadn't realized to what extent she sacrificed. After all, she had let me live with a man who had broken her heart.

"Mom, is a special woman. She is some kind of loving mother," I thought, "to sacrifice her goals for a son who never really appreciated it."

"When did Roy and Heidi marry?"

"It was during the first winter we were living in Bards Crossing."

"You never told me."

"No, as I said; there is still pain."

The remainder of the drive was quiet. After we dropped off Mom, Anne and I headed home.

"Anne, I never guessed what happened between Roy and Mom. I have to look at each of them now with different feelings."

"I think tonight's conversation should not change

anything between you and Roy. It was simply a case of love gone awry between them; it happens. They both put it behind them and carried on. I hope you can do that."

"I know you are right, Anne. I will try."

We continued our drive in silence. However, as I drove, Roy's curious comment about a bloody cross found on Heidi's chest rattled around in my mind. Roy had not given me any details about it, but it was crime information that police usually held back.

I learned much later from Chief Parker that there was a small cross sliced into her breast. This fact was not reported to the press, but after Parker's information to me, I wondered how Roy could have known about it when we talked that day. Of course, Roy had to go to Portland to identify Heidi. If the morgue attendant had pulled the cover lower than her head, he may have seen the cross. It was a question that would nag me for some time.

Chapter Eight

One year later, Roy called me to say that he had sold the farm to a young wannabe dairy farmer. In Roy's words, the kid had more money than brains to take on such a responsibility, but then he had been young once also.

"Roy, you are only in your early fifties. You can have a new life; you can start over; maybe find someone to share the retirement hours."

Roy moved to a Glendale cottage on the lake, but said he would never look for a new mate. It was going to be his and Heidi's place. I thought that to be foolish. However, I kept that to myself.

Eight months later Roy called me to give me some disturbing news.

"Robbie, you know the young man who purchased my farm? Well, he burned it down."

"What?" I said with disbelief, "What happened?"

"I had told him about haying being a dangerous job if not done right. Apparently, he baled the grass when it wasn't dry enough and put it in the hayloft. The damn fool didn't realize that the bales could spontaneously combust. I don't feel sorry for him but my entire herd was killed in the fire. Everything along with the barn and the house you lived in is totaled. It's all gone."

"Roy, I am so sorry. Those animals were a big part of your life."

"I know. I will survive."

"How is life out on the lake?" I asked to break the mood.

"Okay, I have gotten to know my neighbors pretty well. Most are nice. Some have teenage children. I think this place suits me just fine."

"That's great, Roy."

I would call Roy usually once a week to see how he was adjusting to retirement. I thought his retirement in his fifties was not a good idea, especially without Heidi.

He always sounded upbeat. I asked him what he did to keep himself busy; his response made me pause. He said he had taken to late night walks around the lake.

"Yes, Roy, but what do you do in the daytime? Sleep?"

"Oh no, Robbie. I have some skills I am developing."

"What kind of skills, Roy?"

"I have always liked tinkering with things, so believe it or not, I am learning to be a locksmith. I bought a few books and I am taking an on-line course."

"You know that you have to register with the state and get a license if you're going to practice it, Roy."

"I know. I am just doing this for fun. It's doubtful if I will take it beyond the hobby stage."

"Well, as long as your hobby is aboveboard, Roy," I said, ribbing him a bit.

"Of course, of course, Robbie."

Over the next several months, as part of my career plan, I interviewed for a number Chief of Police positions throughout the state. I was starting to lose faith that I would ever get out of Alton. I had made contacts and built relationships with most of the police chiefs in the state. Life hands out opportunity when least expected, sometimes under sad circumstances.

Chief Turner of the Augusta P.D. had a massive heart attack and died. Within the law enforcement community, news such as this travels fast.

My friend, Abner, had heard about it and called me to suggest that I try for the position. With that encouragement, I submitted my paperwork and crossed my fingers.

Of all the places my applications were directed, Augusta was the most promising career-wise, and was the one I truly hoped I would get. It was, after all, my hometown until I was fourteen. It was also a much larger city than Alton with commensurate increases in responsibility and pay for the Chief of Police. By this point in my career, I felt I had enough solid background and experience to manage that position.

When I told Anne, she was not thrilled at the prospect of another move, but being the trooper she is, she supported me.

As luck provided, after several interviews with various department heads, the Mayor, the City Manager, the City Council, along with several public input meetings, I was notified that I had been selected. Police Chief of Augusta!

We immediately began our house search. We found, as the realtor said, "A cute Cape Cod style home with four beds, two baths, a two-car attached garage through a delightful breezeway, a well-manicured lawn with a landscaped patio for those necessary neighborhood parties, and all for an affordable price."

Anne and I fell in love with what we hoped would be our forever home. Being as fumble fingered as I am, I knew that painting the white clapboard sided home with its black shutters would be a farmed-out job. Likewise, as any other repairs would be.

The house was located on a quiet street, Deacon Drive, with lots of youngsters in the neighborhood. We had our dream of adding to the crop of street kids, but our children never happened. Also, it never occurred to me that this home would play an important role in my career as a cop beyond its appeal to us.

Sometimes a person must be careful about what they wish for. After a couple of days on the job, which were spent mostly having to find my way to the men's room, I began a series of meetings with all the subdivisions of the Department to understand the problems and issues which I would have to work.

The Department had the usual division of crimes areas and public information functions. Overall, the department had two hundred patrol officers and a small core of detectives, and a two-person forensics lab. Several of the staff were tasked to manage 911 calls and, as I said, a public information officer to handle snags that sometimes occur.

I was on the job for about six months when detectives informed me that complaints of burglaries in an exclusive area of Augusta were occurring. The Glendale District at the time contained thirty-eight cottages surrounding the shoreline of Glendale Lake, which coincidentally I knew was where my friend Roy had moved. The so-called cottages were very expensive, not only because of their location, but also because they were luxuriously built and maintained.

As for the burglaries, the owners were reporting that someone had entered their homes while they had been away for a few days. Detectives had interviewed and fingerprinted all the owners; taken appropriate photographs and had the doors and windows dusted for prints. Suspicious fingerprints were found around the doors. These were entered into AFIS but there were no matches.

The investigators' reports were disturbing to us because it was apparent that the perpetrator or perpetrators were focusing their attention on the bedrooms. More cause for alarm was that only rooms of the women or female teens in the house were tampered with. However, some owners said that they were not aware of anything that had been taken, but it was clear that bureau drawers had been tampered with.

Detective Raymond Brown was the team-leader investigating the break-ins. Ray had been with the Department for more than twenty years. In his late fifties, he was tending to be somewhat overweight for his six-foot frame, balding, with a gruff exterior, but a person I was finding to have a good heart. He was a no-nonsense type; I felt that he was someone I could depend upon. I had wondered how old-timers such as he would react to working with a younger boss, but in my short tenure, I had not noticed any negativity in that regard.

His assessment of the break-in situation was particularly concerning to me. He believed that the culprit broke into the cottages when the families were not at home, but most alarming, he felt that criminals such as this are never satisfied with just breaking-in.

"Chief, they will keep making changes to their MO by taking greater risks thereby increasing potential harm to the homeowner," Ray warned.

"In what way would the homeowner be at greater risk," I asked.

"By greater risk, I mean that the perpetrator may try breaking in when the owners are there."

"I see, Ray, how long have these break-ins been happening?"

"We had our first call a few months ago. Four more followed shortly afterward."

"Are there any other areas of the city experiencing break-ins?"

"Yes, it's not consistent, though; sometimes we get a couple a week and then nothing for months. You know; the commercial businesses occasionally have problems."

"Right, but no homes outside of Glendale have reported any break-ins?"

"None reported to date."

"Do you have any suspects in mind?"

"There are none that I can say with any certainty. We have interviewed people whose homes are near the ones broken into. We haven't found any red flags, so no, we are at a standstill."

"What is your opinion of the type of person doing this?"

"My thought is that it is a teenager, a loner who is going through some unhealthy fantasies. He is seeking thrills by B&E and focusing on the females of the house."

"Ray, how does this fit with your earlier statement that the perpetrator will take greater risks? Would you expect that of a teen?"

"Yes, I've seen a similar situation in my early days as a detective."

"Ray, are the owners certain that the perpetrator takes nothing?"

"I asked Detective Alissa Riley to assist me with the interviews. I hate to ask teenagers or their mothers how many panties and bras they have. Alissa is able to do that without blushing, or them getting upset."

"Can you ask Alissa to join us?"

"Sure."

Moments later, Detective Riley came to my office.

I had first met Alissa earlier in my "meet and greet" sessions. Alissa was a younger detective, probably about thirty. She had been in the department for six years. She stood about five-eight with shoulder length brown hair. With a slim figure, her weight was appropriate for her height, which told me that she took her health seriously.

Over the past few months, Anne and I had my seven detectives and their spouses over to our home. Alissa stood out as one I would be able to trust. She was not intimidated by authority, especially the political type. Alissa was my kind of detective.

"Alissa, I asked Ray this question; are the homeowners certain that the burglar takes nothing?"

"It isn't clear, Chief. For instance, many of the mothers and teenage girls I talked to have numerous undergarments, that is, pairs of panties and bras. These people are wealthy, so they buy what they want."

"So, at this point we'd have to find this guy to know what has been stolen. Wouldn't you think that the women would know what's missing?"

"You would think. Well, there is one thing this guy does sometimes to scare the household. The bureau drawers are left open. Not always, but we have found that it is are only the women's dresser drawers. He wants them to be afraid."

"Alissa, Ray believes this is the work of a teenager gone amuck. What do you think?"

"I am not sure I agree. Whoever it is, he is good at what he does. Further, he wants to intimidate and hurt people by leaving their bureau drawers open to show them he is able to enter their private space without their permission to make them feel violated. I think that person is not a youngster. I agree with Ray, and am worried that whoever he is, he may want to escalate the thrills."

"Yes, that is what Ray said also. Have we sent out a

warning to the Glendale residents?"

"Chief Turner did not want to upset the residents, so he refused to do it," Ray replied.

"We may be doing a disservice to all our residents. I know that some Glendale residents are on the City Council. How is it they are not aware of the break-ins?"

"They are, they also gave Turner his marching orders," Alissa answered.

"If he escalates his activity and someone gets hurt, who is going to answer for that?" I pushed.

"The thought that the Chief had at the time was we didn't want to alert the burglar that we were watching the area."

"But we still have scared citizens and no suspects. How will we get out of that?"

"Chief, we wanted to let Glendale know."

"When we break up here, I want you to make up a simple flier asking people to lock their doors, and to fix any things that make it possible for someone to get into their homes. Let them know we will assist if they have questions.

"Show me the flier; print up the copies; then I want you two to go to Glendale with the fliers and put them on every door in the District. Understood? I will take the heat from the City.

"In the meantime, I will talk to the Mayor. Let's move quickly on this; we are in a world of trouble if the local papers get their hands on it.

Chapter Nine

My meeting with Mayor Flynn did not go well. His position was purely political; he had been the block behind failing to inform the Glendale residents. Apparently, he was worried about property values and re-election.

He told me not to do what I had planned, so I phoned Alissa and Ray to stop working on the notices. I decided on another approach by calling Margaret Parsons, the local nose for the newspaper.

"Hello, Margaret, this is Chief Connor; you covered my swearing-in ceremony for the *Augusta Post*. At the time, we had a chance to speak about the community and my plans for taking the crime stats down."

"Yes, Chief, I remember clearly; what can I do for you?"

"Anne and I are inviting a few friends over for dinner on Saturday evening. I know this call to you is short notice, but we would like to invite you and your husband over for some steaks, wine and good conversation. We want to assimilate ourselves into the community. Do you think you can make it?"

"Well, it is a rather late invitation; let's see, today is Thursday; I will need to check with Jeff if he has any plans. Thank you. I will get back later today. Is that alright?"

"That is fine, Margaret. I look forward to your call."

That afternoon, the Parsons accepted the invitation for six-thirty; I phoned Anne to let her know.

At the station, I held a strategy meeting with Alissa and Ray.

"I apologize for pulling back on the notice campaign, but politics has forced our hand. We need to continue to cover the Glendale area closely."

"Yes, we haven't received any more calls from Glendale since the Mobley break-in on August 5th. It seems that this criminal is somehow getting information about our patrols," Ray interjected.

"Are we patrolling with unmarked cars, Alissa?"

"Ray is handling that, Chief."

"We are patrolling with marked cars during the day and unmarked at night."

"Do they patrol all night, Ray?"

"Yes, I want two to a car. One is allowed to nap while the other keeps watch, but I can tell it is wearing thin."

"I can understand that. One more thing about the patrols, you know that even unmarked cars are giveaways. They look like police cars."

"Well, Chief, we thought of that; we are using our own cars for some of the patrols, but that can't last. It is putting a strain on the whole department. I've been getting some calls from the wives."

"I understand; it is time to move in a different direction. I alluded to another approach this morning. Can you and your spouses make a dinner at our house on Saturday, say six-thirty?"

"I can, Jim is always looking for things to do on the weekend," Alissa replied.

"I have to check with Mae," Ray answered.

"I truly want you both there; I have another reason for the invitation. Margaret and Jeff Parsons will also be there that evening."

"Chief, you are inviting the press?" Ray asked with disbelief.

"I am. The reason is that we believe this guy will eventually escalate his activities. If we don't warn the residents and someone, God forbid, gets hurt or killed; it rests squarely on our shoulders.

"As you know, stuff rolls downhill, so the City Fathers will claim that they were unaware and we just didn't protect them."

"So, what are your nefarious plans for this 'dinner,' Chief?" Alissa asked.

"Ah, yes, nefarious; I will let it slip that we are dealing with safety issues out in Glendale. I won't tell her too much, but I will ask Margaret to keep this information off the record, knowing full well she probably won't. She will do a bit of snooping and then blow it up into a scoop. That is my hope."

"Won't she out you also?"

"I don't think so. The 'unnamed' source ploy. She will have something on me and will use it in the future. It's a bit of newspaper blackmail. I am ready for that."

"You've got balls, Chief. Sorry, Alissa, didn't mean to offend." Ray blathered.

"It's okay, Ray, I've heard worse."

"My next thought about capturing this criminal is that

we need some outside help. I know we are doing all that we can. We need a profiler to assist. Maybe we can get someone from the FBI."

"Oh, Chief, not them. They will push us right out," Ray exclaimed.

"Ray, I know how they work, but we do need them in this case. It's medicine; bitter medicine, but necessary. Sorry."

"Well, Chief, I trust your judgement. I hope for the best."

"We will need to cooperate with them. If we do, they may help, not hinder. The newspaper story will put great heat on us; I will be able to say that FBI help is on the way. I have already contacted the regional office in Portland. They will send out a rep on Monday."

"Chief, I am nervous that the paper and the FBI stories will force the burglar to stop his activities. Then he gets away," Alissa theorized.

"You may be right, Alissa; Margaret may hold the story, you never know. After the rib-eyes and wine on Saturday, her moral compass may make her honor her agreement.

"If she does print a story, it may scare the perp into inactivity. In that case, it is almost a win-win for us. The problem with that win-win idea is that a dangerous person is still on the loose. But with profiling help from the FBI, we may be able to catch him."

"I don't know, Chief, I'm with Alissa on this. There seem to be too many 'ifs.' Things could go terribly wrong."

"I know; it's a risk that I feel we have to take. In any event, I will shield you two. Plan on Saturday, if you can. It will be fun."

* * *

On Saturday, the party preparations were all set. I had picked up the rib-eyes and wine along with stronger drinks and mixers to break the ice and lube the flow of thoughts. We planned to have the get-together on the patio where people could relax more. This arrangement would be especially critical to keep me involved with our guests while I was cooking the steaks and potatoes on the grill.

Instead of the six people I had invited, there would only be four. Ray had called Thursday evening to give an excuse to not attend. It was not much better than the "broken fingernail" one sometimes hears.

I understood; he was not a risk taker. He was late in his career. If the Mayor and City Council decided to end my tenure because of this scheme, Alissa and he would surely be next to say goodbye.

Margaret and Jeff were the first to arrive. After introductions were completed, I took the drink requests. I appreciated Anne's skill at hosting parties. She soon had the Parsons chatting about a myriad of trivialities.

Margaret, as I had remembered was a tall woman in her early fifties. She had long, bottle-blond hair with roots just starting to show. Her slacks and top fit her body, perhaps a little too tightly. Margaret still had a reasonably good figure, but as she disclosed; she was tending to plumpness, if she wasn't careful. She was cheerful about it saying that two days a week at the gym might help her to regain that look she had years ago.

When she spoke, her husky voice gave away the fact that she was a smoker for probably most of her adult years. Her clothes, though clean, I suppose, had the smell of nicotine. Her face bore the unmistakable appearance of one who has smoked cigarettes for many years. It was clear that Jeff, on the other hand, did not smoke.

I had warned Anne of Margaret's habit, so she dug out old ashtrays no longer used. As you may remember, at one time ashtrays were part of a home's décor.

Through chit-chat, we learned that they had been together for fifteen years, ten of those married. They appeared compatible, finishing up each other's sentences and laughing at the other's silly witticisms.

Jeff, on the other hand, was not at all what I expected. He was fit and hale. He looked to be about fortyish.

"Hmm," I thought, "Margaret, a cougar?"

What they saw in each other wasn't obvious. That they were compatible, at least in social situations, went without saying. I thought them to be people trying to work their way through life like the rest of us, not withstanding my distaste for reporters.

Alissa and Jim arrived at exactly 6:30; took their drinks and made small talk with the Parsons while Anne and I kept the drinks refreshed and prepared to grill up the dinner.

Jim, who had been a guest at our home a few times, was

an ideal match for Alissa. In his thirties, he was already a career success managing a small manufacturing company, which he had started in his mid-twenties.

With the guests relaxing in the comfortable patio chairs scattered about, small talk and stories continued. When Anne suggested that it was time to get dinner started, I put the ribeye steaks and potatoes on the grill. The salad and vegetables had been prepared in advance by her.

Throughout dinner, we continued to make small talk so important to the fluidity of a party. After dinner, the drinks kept flowing; I kept an ear for the silly laughter that occurs when something is not comical, but people laugh anyway. At this point, it was time to make my faux pas.

So, I started, "Alissa have you finished the report on the Glendale break-ins?"

"I don't think that we should…," Alissa said on cue.

"Oh, you are right," I said as though I meant it, "I shouldn't talk business tonight."

"What's this about Glendale break-ins?" Margaret chimed in.

At this point, she had already consumed seven strong Bloody-Mary cocktails. They hadn't affected her at all. I also noticed that Jeff did drink rather heavily over the evening, but scotch and water only.

"They are drinkers," I thought, "Perfect for my scheme tonight."

"I apologize, Folks, I should not have said that. Margaret, would you be willing to forget what I just said?"

"Of course, Robert, we don't want to spoil such a delightful evening with business. My lips are sealed."

I knew that was a flat-out lie. Her reputation as an aggressive reporter was well known, which is why I chose her.

Around 10:30, Alissa and Jim, on cue, broke up the party by leaving. Margaret and Jeff soon followed. As they were departing, I asked Margaret if she would not print anything in the paper about what she had heard.

"Of course, Robert, you can trust me." With that assurance, they drove off.

"I wouldn't trust her as far as I could throw her," Anne said.

"Nor would I. She will begin to snoop around and by Wednesday, I should hear from her. She will ask about some details that she has dug up."

"What will you do?"

"I will play along and give her a few tidbits which are true, but aren't vital to our work. At that point, she will decide to publish her story. I will have succeeded."

"What if she names you?"

"She won't; she'll use the 'unnamed source' charade they all use. That way she will keep me tamed."

"What happens if she doesn't publish the story?"

"It's back to planning, but damned if I know what else to plan."

"I know you, Rob, you will think of something; you always do. It's time for bed," Anne said with a smirk.

Chapter Ten

Several days later, Margaret phoned me during lunchtime.

"I heard that some kid is doing 'panty raids' out in Glendale. Any truth to that, Chief?"

"We think that's the case, Margaret, but we don't know for certain."

"How serious is this situation?"

"Well, we don't want to upset the community at large, but any burglary anywhere needs to be taken seriously."

"Is there any other part of the city affected?"

"Just the usual over in the business district."

"My sources have said that you haven't put out a notice to warn people. Is that true?"

"At this point, that's true, Margaret. Are you going to honor our agreement of the other night?"

"Like you, Chief, I have bosses. They don't like to get scooped by the *Gazette*."

"So, you are going to publish a story?"

"I think I have to, Chief. I'm sorry; I will try to convince them not to."

"Do your best, Margaret, I would appreciate it."

Apparently, she succeeded because no story was published.

On Friday, I received a phone call from the Portland FBI office.

"Chief Connor, this is Agent Patrick Kelly, I am the section chief of the local office. You requested an FBI profiler to assist you for some recent serial break-in cases."

"Yes, Mister Kelly, I did."

"Normally, that request would be handled by Washington directly, but we have an agent here who has worked with the DC Profilers. I am planning to send out Agent Smith on Monday. He is not a profiler. He will assist you with profiling support from DC. Is that acceptable?"

"Yes, any help at this point is welcome."

With that assurance from Portland, I notified Ray and Alissa to set up an office for our visitor to use and to prepare a report covering the facts and our speculation concerning the perpetrator.

Monday morning arrived along with a very pleasant surprise as the FBI agent entered my office.

"Abner, you, old dog, you. So, you're the Agent Smith that Patrick Kelly was talking about!"

"Yes, I asked Kelly to not give you my name. I wanted to surprise you."

"Well, you did that alright, Abner. I'm ashamed that we haven't been in touch as much as we thought we would. I let the daily grind get in the way."

"I'm guilty, too. Time slips away."

"Well, how are you? How is Maryanne?"

"We're fine, Robbie, fine."

"How long have you been stationed in Portland?"

"I got my orders to the Office in January, but I spent four months earlier this year on the west coast working some things out there. Sorry, I can't talk about it. Since I've gotten back, the Portland Office has been overwhelmed with work, so I haven't had time to get together with you."

"I understand, Abner. Gee, it is great to see you. I hope that you and Maryanne can join us sometime for dinner. How long are you going to be with us for this project?"

"Kelly has given me two weeks; we'll re-examine it at that time, if there is a need. I'm sure that you can appreciate that this kind of case isn't a high-level priority for the Bureau. I had heard that you had taken over here, so I pushed for us to help."

"Well, I am so happy that you did. Portland is too far to commute, where are you planning to stay?"

"I'll book a room at the hotel sometime today."

"Why don't you stay with us? I'll phone Anne and let her know. We were talking the other day about you and Maryanne. It's insane how we have allowed time…"

"I don't want to be a bother."

"It's no bother, Abner, we'd love to have you stay with us."

"Let me see what the hotel has before we make plans. Okay?"

"Okay, well, let's get down to business. We have had several breaking and entering cases in one section of the city. I have two detectives working the details. The problem is that we can't decide if what we are facing are teenage pranks, or if we have a more serious problem."

"Either way, Robbie, it is serious, but you know that."

"Yes. That's the reason I called your office; we are

hoping that someone can look at what's going on here. We think it's important to check our assumptions. A profile of the criminal would help tremendously."

"I don't know if Kelly spelled out my role to you. My part here will be to provide a pipeline to the Bureau's profiling group. We have some of the best in the world."

"I know, Abner; what do you need to know?"

"First, it would be very helpful if you could give me a picture of the District. You know, the layout of the area where the break-ins have occurred. Any information you have to help provide a focus of the activity."

"We can provide that," I answered. "What else?"

"I need to know as many details of the break-ins that you have: dates, times, entry specifics: doors, basement windows, etc., articles stolen, any information your intruder inadvertently or purposefully has left behind, witness statements; that should do it for a start."

"The break-ins are in the Glendale Lake District, Abner. None of the houses have basements because they're located on lakefront lots."

"Well, that makes it a little bit simpler."

"My detectives, Ray Brown and Alissa Riley have written up detailed reports which are available. I've set up office space for you. The reports are on the desk. Ray and Alissa will be available for any questions you have."

"Thank you, Robbie. I'll get started now."

With that, I left Abner alone to review the reports. Later in the day he informed me that the hotels were booked for the week because of a convention in town.

"Well, you certainly have to stay with us at least for this week."

"At least let me pay for my expenses, Robbie."

"Nonsense, Abner, you're one of the family. I think that the convention doesn't break up until Sunday; that's the usual day things clear out. Anne and I have to travel to Bards Crossing to help my mother next weekend, so you'll have the whole house to yourself."

"Fine, Robbie, I should have my room at the hotel by the time you return."

"That's fine, Abner, that sounds like it will work out."

"I'd like to get started with the discussion. I read all the reports. We need to review the material as a group before I send it out."

"Right, Abner, let's go to the conference room. Alissa and Ray will present what we know. That should provide a detailed background for us to discuss."

"I suggest that we start with the details of the Glendale District to provide Abner with enough information of the area to help with his report to the Bureau. Alissa, why don't we start with the District map?"

"Okay, Chief," Alissa began. "The first slide is a map of the Glendale Lake District. As you can see, the district is divided into four address quadrants, which makes for confusion at times when we are called to the area."

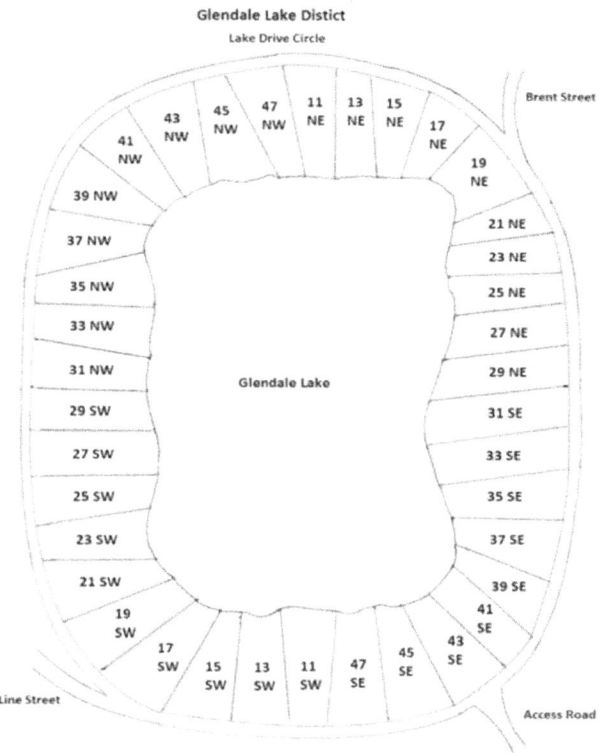

"I can see that. I don't envy you, Folks," Abner said. "What is the terrain of the area?"

"Well, the land slopes gently upward from the lake, probably about twenty-five feet above the lake level, on the average. The Lake itself is about three thousand acres, and roughly circular."

Alissa continued her description.

"Lake Drive Circle, which surrounds the lake cottages, is more than eight miles. The house lots are a couple of acres apiece.

"The Cottages are generally situated centrally on the sites, but the lots run quite a distance from the lake to the road. Therefore, most cottages are not visible from Lake Drive Circle. The lots are heavily wooded, making it easy for someone to travel between the cottages without being noticed."

"Tell me more about the cases you have," Abner said.

"There have been five reported cases of B&E in the Glendale section over this summer. We have a list of the addresses broken into to date. I say to date because until we can catch this person, we assume that we will have more calls to the area."

"What type of homeowner is being targeted? Are they young, old, male, female, single, married?"

"Right now, there seems to be a mix, but if I had to describe the trend, I would say the cases are beginning to lean toward younger women."

"I am starting to believe that your person may be a teenager or college student out of school for the summer."

"That idea is one we have tossed around, but we are worried that whoever it is may escalate his activity."

"Do you have any good suspects at this point?"

"No. Only speculations," I answered

"So, show me the break-in list," Abner pushed.

Glendale District
Lake Drive Circle

NW Section
47 Parks, K.D.
45 White, P.T.
43 West, H.D.
41 Evans, M.R.
39 Sharpe, A.L.
37 Monroe, G.K.
35 Schell, J.D.
33 McCray, K.L.
31 Clay, T.G.

NE Section
11 Green, K.D.
13 Hopper, M.A.
15 Grady, J.M.
17 Rivers, R.W.
19 Cannon, W.T.
21 Hicks, D.A.
23 Savage, L.T.
25 Mobley, F.R.*
27 Newman, J.F.
29 Kelly, E.S.

SW Section
11 Tracy, R.O.
13 Terry, G.D.
15 Walsh, T.M.
17 Parker, T.S.
19 Shay, T.J.*
21 Lester, E.P.
23 Vogel, H.K.
25 Usher, P.F.
27 Brown, D.H.
29 Dent, H.K.

SE Section
31 Hepburn, R.S.
33 Kimble, T.M.*
35 Stevens, A.B.
37 Lenz, R.S.*
39 Burns, D.A.
41 Harley, M.D.*
43 Shaw, R.B.
45 King, R.L.
47 Mosher, H.D.

"Can I assume that the area is tranquil since it appears to be an exclusive neighborhood from your description?"

"It is very quiet out there."

"What about alarm systems? Are the cottages alarmed?" Abner asked.

"The five cottages broken into do not have alarms," Alissa answered.

"That is really stupid. With their money, alarms should be a priority," Abner responded.

"People don't keep dogs out there? It would be very difficult for someone to sneak around the cottages without some mutt barking," Abner remarked.

"That's a good point, I believe there are some dogs in the area, but don't quote me," Ray expressed.

"Well, it's damn foolish; the animals could save their lives," he voiced.

"It's a fluid, rich community; people are constantly coming and going on business, vacations, and who knows whatever else. Conversations I've had with a number of the residents tell me that they think pets are a nuisance, so most don't have them, dogs or otherwise," Alissa answered.

At this point, Ray, who had summarized the five cases, continued with the review.

"These following five cases all occurred when the occupants of the home were away from the premises. This is why we have held onto the view that this criminal is probably a teen or someone who is out for cheap thrills. Of course, Case 5 may show we could be quite wrong for a very serious reason. Here they are," Ray continued.

Case number 1 – # 37 LDC Southeast Section
Owners: Richard and Louise Lenz, ages, mid-fifties
Details: On June 15th, returned from a two-day trip to their daughter's home. Found the back door ajar; Louise's dresser drawers were left open and rifled through. Many intimate items were taken, but they are unsure of how many. Nothing else disturbed or taken from the home.

Case number 2 – # 19 LDC Southwest Section
Owners: Thomas and Maureen Shay, ages, mid-sixties
Details: On June 30th, returned from a week's vacation. Found the bedroom window broken; Maureen's dresser drawers open many of her personal clothes were strewn on the floor. Unsure if any are missing. Nothing else disturbed or taken from the home.

Case number 3 – # 41 LDC Southeast Section
Owner: Michael Harley, age, mid-sixties
Details: On July 8th, Jennifer Harley, age 26, returned from a night at her boyfriend's home to find a window broken. Jennifer is the lone occupant. Her father, Michael, lives in Phoenix, Arizona. Jennifer's dresser drawers were open and many of her personal clothes were stolen. She is unsure how many were taken. Nothing else was disturbed in the home.

Case number 4 – # 33 LDC Southeast Section
Owner: Theresa Kimble, age, mid-forties

Details: On July 9th, Theresa, a nurse, returned from her shift at midnight to find her back door open and as in the other cases, her dresser drawers were not shut. She is unsure how many clothes, if any, are missing. Nothing else was disturbed in the home.

Case number 5 – # 25 LDC Northeast Section
Owner: Frances Mobley, age, mid-forties
Details: On August 5th, Frances, a nurse, returned from a trip to find her back door open. She didn't realize anything was stolen until she opened her dresser drawers. In this burglary, the burglar took time to shut the bureau drawers. Most of her personal undergarments were missing. Since she had been away for a month, we are not certain when this burglary took place. Nothing else appears disturbed in the home.

"This case, as I mentioned before, is different from the first four because the intruder left a letter for MS. Mobley. It is filled with mistakes, which may be done on purpose. Here it is," Ray said.

"That is so juvenile with the phony misspellings," Alissa said.

Hi Frances, I love your body. I wathed you miny nights with yur clothes off. You aren't very carful about closing yur windo shades or locking yur door. I will com over som night when yur are there.

"I agree with your consensus that the intruder may just be trying to hide his identity," Abner interjected.

The slide show continued with interior and exterior photos of the affected homes; statements of the home owners; photos of disturbed areas of the bedrooms, descriptions of clothing articles taken, and photos of the points of entry into each home.

"As you can see, Agent Smith, we don't have much evidence. We have no eyewitnesses, no footprints leading to and from the houses. I can't imagine how the Bureau will be able to profile anyone from this," Alissa added.

"Looking at the entry points, I noticed that for several of the B&E's, the thief entered through doors, which you report did not have defective locks, by the way.

"The profiler can estimate the size of the individual from those cases which the intruder entered through the window openings. If you have measured them, I will add them to your report."

"We did not measure them. I can have someone do that today."

"No, Chief, I think I need to visit each home, so now is a good time to do it."

"Fine. I will have Alissa and Ray accompany you."

Later that week, Abner sent his report with the appropriate information to the Bureau.

Chapter Eleven

Since Abner was staying with us that week, Anne and I had time in the evenings to reminisce with him. For me, it was like old times. I savored every minute. One evening though, the conversation turned serious and personal.

"Robbie, do you remember the brutal murder of Heidi Hepburn that took place in Portland sometime ago? I remember that she and Roy were close friends to you. You had talked about them when you returned from your summer job."

"I do, of course, Abner; Roy and Heidi were my 'foster' parents. I loved them both."

"Do you know what happened?"

"What do you mean?"

"We, I don't mean me, worked with the Portland police to solve the case. It took about a year to identify a solid suspect. The night before the police had planned to arrest the guy, he was found on a side street also brutally murdered; I mean it was brutal. I won't describe it for Anne's sake, but the crime scene and coroner's pictures are horrific."

"I am very surprised, Abner. Chief Parker and I had a conversation after Heidi's murder; he said he would keep me informed if anything developed, but this is the first I've heard that they found a suspect. I hate to ask this question, but did the suspect's murderer ever get caught?"

"Not as of this date. He seems to be charmed. No clues, no suspects, no nothing."

"It's odd. I talked to Roy; you probably don't know it, but he lives in the Glendale section of Augusta. Well, he said that he thought the police never had a suspect in Heidi's death."

"The only thing I can tell you is that the police considered Roy to be a strong suspect for the murderer's murder for quite a while."

"What? I can't believe that. Roy wouldn't hurt a fly!"

"It's true; they had absolutely no evidence, though. One thing happened to make them suspect Roy. Apparently one of the detectives told Roy about the person they suspected killed Heidi. Roy was quiet about the information, but you know what they say about 'the quiet ones.' Change of subject; did you know that Heidi was very wealthy?"

"No, she said that she was from a Midwest town, but nothing about money."

"In fact, she was the daughter of Emile Grant from Chicago. That is where she grew up. He was a shipping magnate whose ships plied Lake Superior carrying iron to the foundries in their heyday.

"She had two brothers who were lost on the Lake. She left Chicago after their deaths. Heidi moved her father to a Portland nursing home when he became too ill to take care of himself."

"What about her mother?" Anne asked.

"I think she died when Heidi was in her teens."

"Christ, Abner, that is sad. Honestly, she never gave any of that away. Roy didn't ever mention it. I still can't believe they thought he was capable of murder."

"A rather extensive background check was done on both of them for different reasons. Roy's parents immigrated to the States from Aberdeen, Scotland two years before he was born. Another sad thing about Roy, his father died several months before his birth, so Roy never knew his father."

At that point, I realized that the FBI check wasn't as good as Abner thought. Roy did finally get to know his father.

"Roy had told me years ago that he had inherited money, which allowed him to purchase the farm in Augusta," I disclosed.

"As far as they could tell, the Hepburn clan had no money; no large insurance policies were found, so the money must have come from Heidi. The money he used to buy the farm was not actually inherited; it was Heidi's money," Abner stated.

"I wonder why Roy lied to me," I thought, "He was so decent to me; I just can't believe it."

"You must know that Roy did inherit a huge amount of money when Heidi died, don't you?"

"Roy often comes over for dinner, but we never talk about money; that wouldn't be right," Anne imparted.

"Well, he did," Abner said.

"Abner, Roy is a solid friend. If he didn't tell me the truth about money that is okay."

"I'm not trying to say that his reluctance to tell you is a

crime, just that there are things about Heidi's murder that raised red flags about them and their relationship.

"For instance, what if Roy hired someone to kill Heidi and then Roy killed him? The secret is safe. You know the old mafia saying: three people can hold a secret as long as two of them are dead."

"God, Abner, that is insane. They loved each other!"

"Nothing is impossible; you know that as a cop. I don't want to say it but someone has to."

"You just said he has been cleared."

"Yes, but unsolved murders are never closed."

"Abner, I know that is right, but you are wrong about Roy."

"Time will tell. I need to turn in. We have a big day tomorrow. We need to make a final pass at the information that I will send to the Bureau."

After we all went to bed, Anne and I lay awake softly talking about what Abner had said that evening.

"Anne, Roy spends time with you sometimes when I am not at home. After tonight's revelations, does that bother you?"

"Rob, Roy has never been out-of-line with me in any respect. If he had, I would have told you. He is our friend; he was like a father to you. How can you turn on him?"

"I'm not, Anne, but he didn't tell me the truth years ago."

"I hate to say it, but so what? He was a much better father to you that the biological one whom you've never met. You owe him some degree of loyalty. Yes, he lied, but I repeat, so what? He watches our home when we go away; he pet-sits our animals without ever asking anything in return. He is our friend."

"Okay, Anne, you make good sense. I love Roy, which is what was so hard to hear what Abner had to say."

"Did you notice that Max had his usual muffled growl when strangers are in the house? He didn't seem to warm up to Abner."

"What I noticed was that Max did not leave your side, but he has been good about meeting people. I didn't think it unusual."

"No, Rob, he generally doesn't act that way."

"Well, he is a dog; who knows how they think? German Shepherds can be unpredictable around strangers. He is partial to you, so I can understand it."

"But Rob, most times he is much friendlier to a stranger after an hour or so, but not tonight. The first time he saw Roy we couldn't keep them apart, Max trusted him right away."

"Roy is used to working with animals and he is not afraid of dogs. You know that dogs sense when someone is afraid of them and they act on it. Who knows why? Abner may be afraid of Max and he knows it."

"Okay, Rob, maybe I'm making too much of it."

"Good night, Love."

"Good night, Rob."

Before I drifted off to sleep, my thoughts swirled with

memories of some things Roy had said to me years ago. His comment about the fate of the man who had shot his first wife: "You can't shoot what you can't see."

At the time, I thought he meant that the man had gone blind for some reason. Was Roy involved with that? His smile when I asked back then now haunts me.

And how about the John Goldie murder? Someone had smashed the skull of the man accused. What did Roy mean with his "What goes around; is what comes around" comment and smile?

And what about Heidi's suspected killer? Someone had horribly murdered him. The police didn't even know if he was Heidi's murderer. How would Roy have known this guy was going to be accused? Oh, right, Abner said that a detective told Roy. It made no sense to me. I resolved to understand my friend, Roy, better.

I would find a way to talk to him about Heidi, John Goldie, and the unfortunate hunter. I would use the powers of my office to get facts of these incidents through the police network. That would have to wait, though.

On Friday, Anne and I left for Mom's home and returned Sunday night. Abner had left our home by then for the hotel.

Abner had tidied up the house; washed dishes; he had even washed and folded the laundry before leaving. Anne and I were pleasantly surprised. What a thoughtful and great guest! Abner, my friend, was more than welcome anytime at our home.

By the next Friday, Abner's two-week commitment to help us was complete.

"I will head back to Portland, Robbie. The Bureau's Profilers have promised to have their opinion, that is, a profile, within two weeks. If you have questions about it, give me a call."

"Thank you for all your help, Abner. We look forward to the profile. Anne suggested that you and Maryanne come stay with us sometime soon."

"Well, we'll see. Maryanne has become a stay-at-home, so getting out takes a good deal of convincing."

"We would really like you two to spend time with us. It's not a polite invitation which neither party expects to happen. We really want you to come. It's only a four-hour drive from Portland."

"Okay, Robbie, I will convince her. Stay in touch and let me know when it is convenient for you two."

Later that evening, Anne and I looked at our calendar commitments for the next months. I phoned Abner with a weekend invitation. The call went to voice mail.

I hadn't noticed that the phone number that Abner gave me was not a Portland area code. It was probably his FBI number or his cell. It didn't matter; he would return my call sometime.

Chapter Twelve

The following week, we received the FBI profile from the Bureau. We had convinced ourselves that the perpetrator was probably a teen whose hormones had overtaken his brain.

Abner had given his opinion that the burglar may be older than a teen, such as a college student on summer break, but probably someone not much older than that. He believed that would be a more likely scenario, but as he said, he was not a profiler.

The report we received shattered our naïve speculation. The profile read as follows:

"The person involved is most likely not a teenager. From the crime data supplied, the perpetrator has the attributes as follows. This person is very organized and skilled.

The Offender's Sex:

The offender is male, without a doubt. Our lengthy experience has not shown women involved with this type of crime.

The Offender's probable Race:

Because the Glendale area is predominantly Caucasian, the offender is most likely the same race as the residents living in Glendale.

The Offender's physical traits:

From the description of the entry points into victims' homes, the offender chooses access points which allow him with a medium frame to obtain admittance. We feel that the offender is about six feet tall, or slightly less in height. He is fit and strong; he is able to work his way through access points which require agility and strength.

The Offender's Age:

We believe that person is targeting women about his same age or slightly younger. From your data, that could put him in his late thirties or early forties. However, our concern is that this person has shown some propensity for attraction to theft of teenagers' underwear. This fact is disturbing to us because it may indicate that the offender is not receiving the same thrills as when he first started this activity. It is this profiler's opinion that it will not be long before the offender will want to experience the power over a victim real time.

The Offender's relationship with women:

Most likely the offender is married or living with a woman. We do not believe that the woman is his mother or is a mother figure.

The Offender's level of education:

The offender may have some college background or has completed a high school education. We believe this because of the taunting letter left at victim number five's home. Although not perfect, the letter shows a better than average understanding of grammar and punctuation. It may be that the offender is trying to disguise his identity by purposely misspelling, etc.

The Offender's residence:

We believe that these break-ins are done by an offender

living within the area of Glendale or close to the Glendale District. The reason for this assumption is that your data shows multiple break-ins to the same residence on successive nights. The offender lives close to that victim's residence. We believe this is true because his presence does not stand out, i.e., his presence in not out of the ordinary.

The Offender's financial means:

Because we believe that the offender is dwelling in the Glendale District, his source of income must be equivalent to the residents' incomes. The homes in the Glendale District are called cottages, but they are relatively expensive. The offender must be able to afford living there using independent wealth or income.

An Overall concern:

This profiler is very concerned that this offender will escalate his activity very soon. As noted under the age category, the thrills of stealing will soon need to expand into a physical acting-out power scenario over a victim. This will result in harm or death to a victim. Every means should be employed to capture this offender as soon as possible.

After reading the profile, I said, "So, we have a male, probably white, strong, tall, lives in the area, maybe married, maybe has some college education, wealthy or has a job which supports him and allows him to have nightly escapades. Anything else?"

"It's a nice profile; I'm not sure what we do with it," Ray said.

"Well, there goes the horny teen theory," Alissa said, stating the obvious.

"Well, I for one still want to believe that the intruder is just a frustrated teen," Ray responded.

"I would like that also, Ray, but it would be burying our heads in the sand, as they say. Whoever it is, we won't know until we catch him."

* * *

As I feared, shortly after we received the profiler's report another break-in was reported at 43 Southeast Lake Drive Circle. The offender had entered the home; surprised the lone occupant; a young woman, Rebecca Shaw, in bed who screamed as he loomed over her. The intruder ran off. She rushed out of the house to spend the night with the next-door neighbor who sensibly called the police.

A patrol car went to investigate the scene with the on-duty detective, Mark Levine, who secured the home after he located and locked the window used by the intruder.

Although terribly frightened, Miss Shaw could give a partial description. The intruder was wearing a black sweatshirt and pants with a mask over his face. He looked strong, was tall. She was not sure of his race. She said that as the intruder left, a motion sensing light in the hallway was triggered, which enraged the man, who turned back to face the woman. He said he would kill her if she called the police.

Detective Levine specifically noted in his report that nothing in the house looked disturbed.

The next morning, Ray went to the burgled home. As he went into her bedroom, Ray realized that the prowler had returned that night after Detective Levine had left the scene because bureau drawers were now open and appeared rifled.

He saw a letter placed on the chest of drawers. It was typed with no misspellings, and the intent was clear. It read:

I promised to kill you if you called the police. Too bad you left I will be back to have fun with you.

Ray put the letter into an evidence bag; sealed it; and placed it into his car. He planned to show it at the team's next meeting, but not to the victim.

Ray knew that if the woman had remained in the house, he would be investigating a homicide, not a burglary.

Ray then asked the woman to come back to the home to see if anything had been taken. When she entered her bedroom, she began to cry and shake, but examined the drawers as she was asked to do. She said that some lacy bras, camisoles, and underwear were missing. She could not say how many were stolen. What she did not say was that some personal items were also missing.

Ray told the woman that in her frantic condition, she might have been mistaken about the state of the bureau drawers the night before. She was adamant that the drawers were shut when she went to the neighbor; Ray did not tell her the intruder had returned that night, nor about the letter.

"Is there anyone who can stay here with you?" Ray asked.

"My fiancé is going to live here until we get married. Then we are moving out. I will sell the place; I won't stay here any longer than I have to."

When Ray returned to the station, I said, "I want to increase the night patrols in Glendale. Alissa, I also want a complete update of the list of residents, both owners and renters, if any, who are living in the District."

"I have verified the list to make certain that it is up to date. Many of the cottages are occupied by the original owners, but some of the cottages have been handed off to the owners' grown children living there with their families.

"The point I am trying to make is that there is a mix of older and younger people in the District. I hope this guy doesn't change his MO and start targeting the younger ones," Alissa said.

"Well, young or old, we have to catch him before he tires of whatever is thrilling him these days. We know he is getting more dangerous; ramping up his thrills; the Profilers have said as much; this last break-in clinches it," I reminded them.

"Daring to enter a home, which he knows is occupied, is an escalation of his activity," Alissa added.

"I agree, Alissa; the problem is we can't be certain he bumbled this break-in," Ray voiced.

"Let's not speculate too much, Folks. It doesn't really

help us much. We have to nail this guy before he physically injures someone."

"Give me a minute, Chief. I have it on my desk."

When Alissa returned, I said, "I must say, Alissa, you make my job much easier."

"Thank you, Chief. I've asterisked the six addresses broken into.

"Before we look at the list, Chief, I have to show you the letter that I found at Rebecca Shaw's place. Notice that there are no spelling errors," Ray revealed.

"This guy is pure evil," Alissa exclaimed.

"I wonder what the profiler would say about this second letter to a victim. He isn't trying to disguise his education," I added.

"What could that change mean, Chief?" Alissa asked.

"I don't know, but it can't bode well for us. It's as though the intruder knows we are helpless," I answered.

"Change of subject, Chief. What happened to the story the *Post* was going to print?" Ray asked.

"When I phoned Margaret to thank her for holding off her story, I got a surprise, she never wrote it. Apparently, she didn't quash her story; someone else did it."

"What do you mean?" Alissa asked.

"She said that the publisher received a call from some government person asking not to publish any stories about the break-ins."

"What? That's criminal after the latest incident," Alissa huffed.

"Was it the Mayor who intruded?"

"Margaret said she thought it wasn't him. He didn't know of our plan, but since I had asked him about notifying the Lake people with our notices, I wouldn't put it past him; however, he wasn't aware of our plan, so who could it be?"

"Alissa, please keep going."

"The one at 43 LD Circle Southeast on the list is double asterisked because, as you know, the woman, Rebecca Shaw was home at the time. That could have been a different type of crime scene. Here are the details," Alissa continued.

Case number 6 – # 43 LDC Southeast Section (Serious)

Owner: Robert Shaw, age, mid-forties

Details: On September 18th, Rebecca Shaw, his daughter who is a college student, returned from a late-night party. I'll briefly repeat the details as we have been over this break-in before. The perpetrator broke in by unlocking back door. She screamed when he came to her bedroom and he ran out. She gave a brief description of him, but he had on a mask, and dark clothes covering his arms, so she couldn't tell his race.

"Is there a leaker in the Department?" Ray asked.

"I sincerely doubt it, Ray. Anyway, who would you suspect? In the meantime, let's review the list again," I directed.

Glendale District
Lake Drive Circle

NW Section
47 Parks, K.D.
45 White, P.T.
43 West, H.D.
41 Evans, M.R.
39 Sharpe, A.L.
37 Monroe, G.K.
35 Schell, J.D.
33 McCray, K.L.
31 Clay, T.G.

NE Section
11 Green, K.D.
13 Hopper, M.A.
15 Grady, J.M.
17 Rivers, R.W.
19 Cannon, W.T.
21 Hicks, D.A.
23 Savage, L.T.
25 Mobley, F.R.*
27 Newman, J.F.
29 Kelly, E.S.

SW Section
11 Tracy, R.O.
13 Terry, G.D.
15 Walsh, T.M.
17 Parker, T.S.
19 Shay, T.J.*
21 Lester, E.P.
23 Vogel, H.K.
25 Usher, P.F.
27 Brown, D.H.
29 Dent, H.K.

SE Section
31 Hepburn, R.S.
33 Kimble, T.M.*
35 Stevens, A.B.
37 Lenz, R.S.*
39 Burns, D.A.
41 Harley, M.D.*
43 Shaw, R.B.**
45 King, R.L.
47 Mosher, H.D.

"The Profilers believe that the burglar lives in the Southeast section. I believe that he could live in the

Northeast or Southwest sections as well," Ray pushed. "It doesn't make sense to rule out those two sections."

"I see your point, Ray, but these Profilers make their living by being able to sort through the sort of ambiguities we have. They are professionals with an accurate track record."

"I grant you that, Chief, but the distances between the houses are not that great, and the dense woods make it easy for someone to hit a place and hide. I'm just saying."

"Your argument is noted. Let's move on. I need to give Agent Smith a call; he may know something about the quashing of Margaret's story."

Chapter Thirteen

With Alissa and Ray present, I dialed Abner's FBI number with the speaker-phone on.

"Hello, Abner, Robbie here. A reporter from the *Augusta Post* told me recently that they were told not to print any stories about the Lake burglaries. You know anything about that?"

"I was going to call you; the Section Chief has requested it. We are working a case, which a story about the burglaries would endanger. I can't say anything more about it."

"I understand that, but we are risking people's lives."

"Oh, I don't think that is true, Robbie. From the review we did, I don't think your burglar wants more than panty trophies for his effort. I haven't changed my mind that the culprit is more than a college aged kid trying to get thrills from women's things. Of course, I'm not a profiler, so…"

"I hope you are right, Abner, but he did strike at a home when the woman was there."

"Maybe he made a mistake thinking the house was not occupied. Did he hurt her?"

"No, but he could have. He scared the hell out of her, so I say he did hurt her. Also, he left a threatening letter saying that he would be back."

"Well, I'm sorry, Robbie. We must hold all stories; our case is big. That is all I can tell you."

"Is the FBI going to cover us if the Glendale burglar murders someone?"

"You know that I can't make any kind of promise such as that. Let's hope nothing happens before we finish our case."

"How long will that be, Abner?"

"I can't say anything more, but it won't be for a while."

"Okay, Abner, if anything changes, you must let us know immediately."

"Will do, Robbie. Please say 'hi' to Anne."

"Okay, Abner, thank you."

After the call ended, we continued our conversation.

"Who the hell does the FBI think they are?" Alissa said heatedly.

"I know, I know; we have to do it their way, though. If not, the Mayor will be having our heads."

"He'll probably do that anyway, Chief."

"And when someone gets killed, the whole county will be after our heads," Alissa said, totally frustrated.

"Chief, I've been thinking about the six cottages that were broken into. When we interviewed the residents, everyone insisted that they lock their doors and windows at night," Ray exclaimed.

"Where are you going with this?"

"If that is true, you would think they lock up when they go away. Yet, when they returned from wherever, they find someone has entered their homes and had a field-day with momma's panties."

"What's your point, Ray?" Alisa interrupted.

"Of the six break-ins, how many were forced-door

entries?" I probed.

"Believe it or not, there were none. There was no evidence of forced entry. Only one of the six entries was through a window and that was Shaw's cottage," Ray answered.

"That is unbelievable! They are not locking their doors at night?" I interjected. "I thought you just told me that they said that they always lock their doors and windows at night."

"Well, it isn't surprising, Chief, people are often stunned to find they didn't lock their doors when they get up. I know it happens in my house sometimes."

"Well, if the doors are locked, how is this guy getting in without smashing the doors in?" Alissa asked.

"Either the intruder is skilled at unlocking doors and windows, or the residents are mistaken," Ray responded emphatically.

"I doubt that they are not locking their doors," Alissa retorted. "Women are usually very concerned about that."

"Yeah, I guess I doubt that also," Ray said.

"Then the evidence leaves us with two options to consider. One is that people are stupidly leaving their doors and windows unlocked, or secondly, our burglar is able to jimmy locks open."

"Chief, there is no doubt that this guy is wily, skilled, and a risk-taker. He is taking advantage of peoples' inherent trust in the safety of their neighborhood."

"It may be, but we need to check on a couple of things.

First, if Agent Smith's theory is right, we need to find out if any college students live in the District and if there any people in the District are licensed or trained as locksmiths," I instructed.

"Okay, Chief, we can get on that."

"The FBI profile indicated that our intruder was strong and fit; do we still believe that is necessarily true?" Alissa questioned.

"It may not; if he is able to unlock doors, what strength is needed for that?" Ray answered.

"Not much, obviously."

"Okay, Folks, we need to consider his motivation. Think about this: whatever drives him, may force him to escalate his activities. That means he must include a person, a helpless person, as part of his break-ins to intensify his thrills."

"Exactly, when he has power over someone, this thrill would be greater than his warped need to steal undergarments," Ray added.

"Chief, that means he has to be strong enough to overcome a victim. If what we are saying is true, then the Profilers are correct," Alissa asserted.

"What is worrying me more about the Rebecca Shaw home intrusion is that I have this nagging feeling that that night was the start of his need to seek greater excitement."

"I agree, Chief, with the assault on Rebecca, he was looking to ramp up his excitement. I fear that someone is going to get severely hurt, raped, or even killed."

"I have no doubts that you are correct, Alissa, but…"

"I wish Rebecca Shaw could have given us a bit more of a description of the intruder," Ray interrupted.

"Well, given the trauma she had, I think she gave the best she could. Thank God for the hallway light or we wouldn't even have that," Alissa sympathized.

"Let's talk about the Glendale Lake area. It's about time I spent some time out there."

"You've had your hands full getting used to Augusta and this job, Chief. We all understand," Alissa said.

"If I remember correctly from the city map, aren't there many side roads into the woods on the opposite side of Lake Drive?" I probed.

"They aren't specifically mapped, because they are not roads. They're just openings where cars can pull into the woods. Some of them go rather deep; out of sight of the main circle road," Ray added.

"That's true, kids go parking at night," Alissa said. "I can remember some nights there myself, before marriage, of course."

"Kids still go parking?" I questioned, "Don't they just use each other's bedrooms when the folks are away?"

"They seem to like the woods, along with couples just wanting to get away from the spouses. The places are littered with cigarette butts, beer bottles and condoms. It isn't much fun for the troopers to patrol," Alissa vented.

"I guess nothing's changed from my days of dating."

"Chief, another question we have to answer is this:

where do we think the intruder's comfort zone is?" Alissa stated.

"Let's review where the break-ins are happening. The burglar must be comfortable somewhere in the central area of those break-ins."

"Okay, one break-in is in the Northeast section, four are in the Southeast section, and one is in the Southwest section," Ray reported.

"So, there are none in the Northwest section?"

"Not a one so far, Chief."

"That may mean the intruder lives in the Northwest section and doesn't want to soil his own nest, or he lives in the Southeast section and hits the cottages closest to him. That satisfies the 'comfort zone' issue you brought up," Alissa pronounced.

"That may be, but it doesn't rule out that the culprit may live in the Southwest section, either."

"That's right, Chief, it could be," Alissa answered.

"The Northwest section hasn't reported problems, so we should check to see if the reason is that some cottages there have dogs or alarms; it would back up your earlier point, Chief," Ray added.

"Since the Shaw break-in, things have been quiet. Maybe that close call scared him off," Alissa said.

"Damn, I wish Margaret had published her story."

"I've got to believe that the rumor mill must be working out there anyway, Chief. People must be aware of what's going on," Alissa voiced.

"Maybe so, but I am going back to the Mayor and again ask for permission to… No! I am not; I would rather beg for forgiveness than ask for permission!"

"That's dangerous, Chief, it could mean you know what."

"I know; I just can't depend on the rumor mill to alert the Glendale folks. I have to act. Get the handouts ready; I will mail them out to every address in Glendale. Just because I might get fired doesn't mean you have to."

That evening, I did something I try not to do. I involved Anne in the details of the Glendale case to get her perspective, and to let her know that I may be out of a job shortly.

"Anne, I haven't talked with you much about the Glendale case since our little party with Margaret Parsons."

"I've been expecting to see her story, but I guess your little ruse didn't work," Anne replied.

"No, it didn't, Love; it wasn't that she honored her word which prevented it, though."

"Oh, what was it?"

"The Portland FBI Office got involved and stopped it."

"Why? How did you find that out?"

"I called Abner and he said they have a big case, but he wouldn't say what it was, so I have no idea why that should make a difference."

"So, what's really bothering you?"

"I have made the decision to send notices to the Glendale residents with the intruder warning. The Mayor has specifically ordered me not to do that. I'm putting them in the mail tomorrow. It probably means I'll be fired."

"I don't believe he has the right to fire you over that, Rob."

"I am disobeying an order that both he and the Police Commissioner gave me. Knowing his reputation, he will."

"Well, that'll be a life change, but you know, Darling I am always with you. Do what you need to do. Politics be damned."

"There is one other thing bothering me. I want your opinion about what I should do next. You know that Roy lives in the Glendale area. In fact, he lives in the Southeast section, where most of the break-ins are occurring."

"What does that mean?"

"I haven't mentioned to my detectives that Roy is a good friend, for obvious reasons. We have been discussing the idea that the intruder may live the area, in his comfort zone. Whoever it is, we feel he must be a resident of the district. He is unsuspected by neighbors, so he can burgle cottages, which are short distances from his home. He is familiar to his neighbors and his knowledge of the community allows him to move about the area unnoticed.

"Here's my problem; sooner or later, one of my detectives is going to say that Roy should be a suspect because his cottage is in the midst of the break-in area."

"So, what, that doesn't mean he's involved."

"Not necessarily, but that fact, coupled with his telling me some time ago that he was learning locksmith skills.

That has gotten me to thinking. It makes me wonder; I know it would make the detectives wonder."

"No, Rob, you know who Roy is. He isn't that kind of person."

"Yes, but that makes this so hard to consider. He's been my mentor, my friend, my foster father; he loved and loves my mother. I love him for all those things. He has always been a huge part of my life. Unfortunately, with all the work of this job lately, I haven't been able to stay in contact with him. I don't know what he's up to these days."

"I think you are way off base about Roy. You can't think ill of him."

"I may be off base, but I wouldn't be doing my job as a cop, unless I consider everyone, especially in Glendale, as a possible suspect."

"I don't envy you, Rob; don't forget that Roy is family."

"I know you are right, Anne, but…"

Later as we were relaxing in the living room, Anne turned to me and said, "Rob, this discussion tonight has upset my conscience. I have been delaying telling you something, which has been bothering me for some time."

"What is it, Sweetheart?"

"You remember awhile back that we had Roy watch the house for a week when you and I went to your Chief's Conference in New York. We left Max with him."

"Yeah, Roy often house-sits for us when we can't take Max."

"I know that's… Well, I hate to admit this, but when we returned home, something seemed different."

"What do you mean 'different?' "

"I don't know; maybe I'm confused, but before we left for the conference I had a small load of clothes ready to wash, but I didn't get to it before we left.

"At first, I didn't notice it; later the realization hit me that the dirty wash load was not in the hamper. Then I thought Roy may have washed them, and put them back in my dresser drawer. That would have been like him. He is family.

"Because Roy is Roy, the thought that he might have done that did not offend me, although it made me a bit nervous. No woman likes to think that someone other than her husband is handling her personal things."

"Yeah, it doesn't make me feel good, either, but as you say, Roy is Roy."

"That's not all, Rob. You remember awhile back when he stayed at the house while we went to Mom's?"

"Yes, but what about it?"

"When we returned, I thought I had left a couple pairs of underwear and a bra there. I called her to let her know; she searched, but she said they weren't there. I was confused, and thought I must have thrown them out accidentally."

"How do you throw out underclothes accidentally?"

"Well, that's just it; I have so many bras and underwear that I could be wrong about this. It may not be a big deal, so I've tried to let it go."

"I don't know what to think, Anne. Are you positive about this?"

"That's just it, Rob, I'm not, but it has been on my mind, especially because I didn't say anything at the time. I am probably wrong; it may be just my imagination."

"I think the only thing we can do now is to be more aware and keep track of things."

"Knowing how much we love Roy, the idea of this has bothered me. I am sorry that I didn't mention this earlier, but I wasn't sure. I'm still not."

"Thank you for telling me; try to not let it bother you. We will get to the bottom of this."

With that, we dropped the subject, but now her concerns became mine and they rattled around in my brain. Also, I had purposely not told Anne about Roy's skill as a lock smith.

The next morning, I sent two patrol cars to hand-deliver the notices to the homes in the District. My conscience was clear, almost.

Chapter Fourteen

I say, "almost," because the conversation with Anne increased my doubts about Roy. There were a few matters about Roy which had puzzled me for years. In all the time that I had known and worked with Roy, we never had the opportunity to discuss certain questions I had about his early life.

Nevertheless, there were a few deep, personal events in his life that Roy did share with me, but the stories lacked details, which simply triggered further questions in my young mind. I wanted Roy to explain more, but these were not questions that I could raise as a young person.

Possibly, during those few moments, he let his rigid control temporarily slip, only to catch himself before he said too much. Perhaps, however, Roy felt that what I wanted to know really was none of my business. I admit that I wanted to pry into areas which I shouldn't have. The fact is that Roy wasn't my blood relative; he was not my father, regardless of what I wanted.

As I have noted before, Roy was a reserved man who didn't freely share his personal thoughts. This mannerism was especially important to me because he represented a father figure. No, he was more than a father figure. He was, in fact, my father in many ways. However, Roy kept a distance with everyone, including me, perhaps especially me.

If I am being too judgmental here, it is because Heidi was the exception in his life. I understood that, but as I grew older, it hurt to realize that Roy's nature could not let me into his world as deeply as I would have liked, a would-be father or not. I detest secrets between true friends. If Heidi had not broken a trust with him to tell me about Roy's paternity, most likely, I would never have known that.

Sadly, now that we were both older, the right time or setting to bring questions up had never happened. Even an occasional dinner with me hasn't broken the ice.

I feel shame and a sense of guilt that I have let my imagination fuel a distrust in the one man who was good to me for so many years. The question is this: Was Roy involved with dispensing justice? I need to know, but I also know that the answers will not ever come from Roy.

I need to ask him for more information about death of his first wife. When he had mentioned it years ago, I was too young to fully understand the pain he must have felt, and the strange story of what happened after her death.

The murder of John Goldie gave rise to another situation which I felt needed much more explanation. It seemed serendipitous that with this death also; somehow a sort of wild-west justice had occurred. I wanted to ask Roy for any facts that he might have.

Finally, the murder of our beloved Heidi was so heinous that a heart-to-heart discussion with Roy would be too tough on both of us.

You may ask at this point, why the omission of details of the strange outcomes related to the murder cases which affected Roy's life are important to this story. As a youth, they were only important to satisfy my curiosity, and my need to have Roy's trust. However, at the time of the burglaries in Augusta, the lack of those details cast doubt on Roy and reached to the heart of Roy's character.

To get answers to these nagging uncertainties, I felt I had no choice but to put on my police hat and act. So, using all my contacts with within the law enforcement community, I wanted to get information about these cases, which was otherwise not available to the public. What is more important, I wanted to know if my suspicions about the degree of Roy's involvement with "justice" meted out to the accused murderers were valid. I will relate the facts as I now know them.

Years earlier, Roy had told me that he and his first wife were on a hunting trip when a trigger-happy hunter fired a shot at something that he clearly didn't identify. After hearing the gunshot, Roy found his wife, Lisa, bleeding badly. When the "hunter" came running to see what he had shot, Roy was so enraged he told the "hunter" that he was going to kill him, but Roy controlled his temper, and carried his injured wife out of the woods, but it was too late. She died in his arms. The police charged the "hunter" with manslaughter and Roy for the deadly threat.

The "hunter" hired a lawyer who somehow had gotten the manslaughter charge dropped. He walked out of court a free man. Roy was incensed at the injustice. Later, Roy's charge was also dropped.

A year later, the "hunter" was in a bar in his hometown until late in the evening. As he walked through the parking lot to his car, someone approached him, and threw acid into his face. The acid blinded him.

The case file revealed that the police believed Roy, because of his anger at the man, had been the attacker, but there was no solid evidence to charge him. The assailant was never caught.

When I rummaged through my memory of Roy's version of the story, his well-known smile and his statement, "You cannot shoot what you cannot see," lends unsubstantial credence to Roy's involvement.

The murder of John Goldie was traumatic for Roy. An old man brutally killed for a few dollars was senseless and heartless. As I said earlier, Roy was particularly devastated. I know that Roy had respect and love for the old man who worked hard all his life and asked for nothing. Worse, someone had killed the father Roy had come to finally know. I now believe that Roy was affected beyond the outward showing of grief at the time. Something deep and sinister had changed him.

I never doubted that the thug who beat John to death had been rightly accused by the Augusta police. I only had to look at our case files. Ray Brown was a detective at the time. His reports and records were clear. Ray believed that the drifter was the killer. He was arrested and charged. The problem was the Grand Jury refused to issue a True Bill, so the killer was released. Foolishly, he refused to leave the city and someone was waiting.

Later, the drifter's body was found beaten to death. No one was ever caught for his murder. Again, Roy's smile and statement that "What goes around; is what comes around," haunts me. I can't bring myself to ask Ray, my detective, who he believes was the possible avenger. The case file is irritatingly silent.

The murder of Roy's wife and my beloved Heidi is the saddest one of all. Heidi, a sweet, faithful, and caring friend, was brutally slain. Roy's pain, mine, and all who knew and loved her wanted to avenge her horrible murder. Someone did. The Portland police have no idea who it could be.

After the murder of Heidi's "killer," Roy said, "I hope the bastard rots in hell. What goes around; is what comes around." At the time he said it, it was unsettling and remains so in my mind to this day.

I have shared none of my personal information about Roy with any of my professional contacts. I know that is wrong, but Roy is my friend. I will not do anything, which leads to something that I will not be able to control. He is my friend!

There is also one thing about Roy that is so trivial that I feel ashamed to mention it to you, but for completeness, I will. The issue here was money and a lot of it. About the time Heidi came to Roy's farm, he began spending significant money on the farm. At the time, he led us, Mom and me, to believe that he had inherited it. It was not true.

The question is why would Roy lie to us about inheriting a large amount of money? I am sure the answer is pride. Clearly, Heidi was a partner in the lie for the man she loved. As I said earlier, it was not important to me, but...

In discussions with Abner, he believed that Roy's inheritance of Heidi's sizeable estate was something not so trivial. He felt that the Portland police had not given enough weight to that as a possible motive for murder.

I know that Abner is a good cop, but I argued with Abner that his idea was nonsense talk, which I rejected, as well as the Portland police had. Abner was, however, adamant in this view.

I know Roy, and that it would be impossible for him to murder Heidi. I told Abner that he should be quiet because he was FBI and not involved. That did not help.

Still, that evil idea could not be shaken from my thoughts. Worse, there was a good chance of rupturing lifetime friendships by offending both Abner and Roy for different reasons. I felt that I had to downplay Abner's idea and to never approach Roy with such nonsense. In fact, little did I realize that the situation would eventually be out of my hands.

Chapter Fifteen

In the meantime, I and my crew had a pervert to capture. His latest cruelty, was heralded within a week by a late night 911 emergency call.

"911 Dispatcher; what is your emergency?"

"This is David Hicks at 21 Lake Drive Circle Northeast; my next-door neighbor, Linda Savage just came running over to my house. She is hysterical; crying; almost no clothes on."

"Can you tell me what happened to her?"

"She said a man attacked her. Please, please send the police out to 23 Lake Drive Circle immediately."

"Is the attacker still there?"

"She says, no."

"I am dispatching the police and ambulance now. Stay on the line until they arrive."

"Okay."

"Can she describe her attacker?"

"No, she's crying hysterically."

"I can hear her; put her on the line."

"She won't take the phone."

"All right, stay with me. The police should be arriving now. Stay on the line."

"Thank you."

Moments later, a patrol car arrived along with the ambulance. The duty night detective, Howard Jones, was dispatched to the address to assume jurisdiction of the scene.

The next morning Ray, as senior detective, assumed responsibility of this latest case after receiving reports from Howard and the patrol officer.

Ray and Alissa came to my office to update me.

"How is the lady doing?"

"Not well, Chief, we had her taken to Memorial. The rape counselor and Alissa met with her and a rape kit was completed," Ray answered.

"Was she able to talk last night, Alissa?"

"Very little, the emergency doctor sedated her after we had a brief session with her. She was in bad shape. It looked like she had been in a strangle-hold. She also had a few bruises on her arms."

"Case number seven is a much more serious type with his victim physically involved. The perpetrator is escalating his activities," Alissa interrupted.

"Yeah, Folks, this is what we feared from the beginning of this mess," I added. "Ray please continue."

Case number 7 – # 23 LDC Northeast Section (Serious)

Owner: Linda Savage

Details: September 25th. We don't have many details at the moment except that Linda is twenty-six, and works at the University.

"A curiosity question, how can she afford a cottage out there?" I asked.

"Her parents have both passed away and she inherited it

a few years ago," Ray answered.

"Alissa, even though the hospital said she was not raped, was a rape kit administered?"

"It's standard procedure, Chief," she responded.

"Then I assume that the rape kit will be negative."

"Not necessarily, Chief, she has a fiancé, so…"

"Oh right, she has a fiancé. Make sure we check the results. If they've had sex, we must know about it, because I don't want any 'gotchas' to give some lawyer a chance to get the criminal off."

"Okay, Chief, I will follow up. I would like to discuss a bit more about the two women who were home at the time of the break-ins."

"What do you mean, Ray?"

"I'll get right to the point. They are both pretty, young, have great looking bodies and look very much alike with their long brown hair."

"So, you're saying that these two were stalked by him?"

"I don't think it is a coincidence that these two were selected. My suspicion is that he will go after others with that same look. He must be casing the area, perhaps on weekends when they are home, say out working in the yard or perhaps, sunbathing. The lots are wooded and the cottages are centered on these lots. It would be easy for someone to hide in the brush and spy on neighbors."

"I have suspected that for some time."

"So, you are proposing that the intruder is someone who lives in the Southeast section?"

"I do, Chief. Notice that most burglaries have occurred in the Southeast section."

"Yes, but how can you be so sure?" I asked, trying to deflect the idea that the Southeast section was the only logical place the burglar could live.

"The Profile implies it, and the fact that the intruder has to be able to move on foot from house to house without being noticed."

"Okay, I can see that, but the other side of Lake Drive Circle is densely wooded. Couldn't the intruder drive a car to one those 'parking spots' that errant couples and teenagers use?"

"Sure, Chief, but that only strengthens my argument. If residents are used to seeing a particular resident's car, they may think nothing of it. Plus, these 'parking spots' as you call them, extend pretty deeply into those woods; that suggests they are out of sight from the road."

"I can understand that, but that would mean crossing the road. Surely, someone would notice."

"Not necessarily, Chief, people are very unobservant as you know from your years in law enforcement. Unless something out-of-the-ordinary becomes associated with a parker, people don't notice."

"Well, that could mean the person may live in any of the sections, or doesn't live in the District at all. Sorry, Folks," I argued.

"Then why are the house breaks focused to the District?" Alissa snapped.

"Because that area is the easiest, least patrolled in the City," Ray answered.

"May I say that our logic is becoming circular?" I exclaimed.

"Okay, Chief, perhaps I am too single-minded about my idea." Alissa said, giving up her side of the dispute.

"Alissa, I do think that the intruder does live close to the District or just outside of it. I want to make certain that we don't become too focused to one idea, that's all."

"I understand, Chief, it is hard to tell at this point."

"Ray, to your earlier point, have we increased the patrols in the District?"

"We have, Chief, I've arranged for patrols every two hours during the night from dark to dawn. We also patrol three times a day during daylight hours," Ray answered.

"Good, thank you, both. I wish I knew how we could stop this guy," I uttered, completely frustrated.

"We'll keep working it, Chief."

"One last thing, in line with our policy, neither woman's name is to be given to the public nor the unusual details about the thefts. Our flyers only indicated that residents should lock their doors and windows because of burglaries in Augusta. I want it kept that way."

"Okay, Chief, we have given out very few details to date. None of the unusual things."

"Good, keep it that way."

"Alissa, do you know if Miss Savage is in any shape this morning to get her statement?"

"I checked with the hospital earlier; the duty nurse said that she is awake and much calmer this morning, so I will go back and see."

"That's good. We need her story as soon as possible. Why don't you head to Memorial after we are done here?"

"Okay, Chief, I'll record her statement."

"Ray, has a search of her house been completed?"

"Almost, we are still taking some fingerprints on the doors and windows. Outside the cottage, a partial shoe print was found; we've taken a plaster cast. Howie is contacting a forensic specialist to identify the make and style."

"Ray, after Alissa returns from the hospital, I think it's time we did a detailed summary of the Glendale break-ins."

"I agree, Chief. I'll get started. Let me know when Alissa gets back."

After they left my office, I could not banish the nagging thoughts that Alissa had expressed about the possible location of the intruder's home. Since neither Alissa nor Ray knew of my past life nor past social connections, neither had remarked about the owner's name at number 31 LDC Southeast having any importance.

I began to doubt myself. We all thought that this pervert would do something beyond the clothing thefts, but I had done nothing except sending some flyers to alert residents. Most of those had probably gone out with the day's trash. We had increased the patrols in the area, but had I done enough?

Three hours later, Alissa came to my office accompanied by Ray.

"Chief, I think the best way for me to update you is for us to listen to her statement directly. Do you have time now?"

"Of course, Alissa, let's hear it."

Our review of the taped interview began.

Chapter Sixteen

"Linda, I'm Detective Alissa Riley. Do you remember me talking to you last night?"

"I'm not sure. There were so many people here."

"Well, I am here today to ask you about what happened last night. Do you think you can do that?"

"I'll try, but thinking about what he did to me makes me scared all over again. I might break down uncontrollably."

"I understand; take your time. We are in no rush. This is very important for us. We want to help. Is it acceptable if I record this?"

"I guess it's okay."

"Thank you. Linda, can you tell me anything about him physically?"

"Not really, because it was dark. He flipped me over onto my stomach and blindfolded me, so I didn't have a chance to look at him. He was very strong; his hands felt like iron when he grabbed me and placed me into various disgusting positions. I can tell you he wore gloves."

"Do you think you could identify his voice?"

"Maybe, he spoke slowly and it was low pitched."

"Was there an accent or other characteristic that you detected?"

"To be honest, I was so scared that I didn't really notice. I thought he was going to rape and kill me. My mind was racing and I was crying."

"You're doing great, Linda; can you tell me what happened?"

"Where should I start?"

"You can start wherever you want. If you can…"

"Okay. Last evening, I got home from work and made dinner for myself. Around nine o'clock I called my mother. She and my father are in San Jose, California. They have a beautiful house out there. They own the cottage here also.

"We talked for a few minutes. I wanted to tell her I was planning to visit them next week. I have some vacation time to use up. Then I called Ron; he's my boyfriend, to ask him to stay at the cottage while I was away. I have a kitty.

"At around ten o'clock, I took a shower and dressed for bed. I remember that I had a feeling I was being watched, but shook it off. I checked the locks on the front and back doors and the windows. The flyer you sent out has made me very nervous.

"I got into bed and read for a few minutes before I put out the light and went off to sleep. Suddenly he was on top of me, choking me. I couldn't breathe.

"He told me not to struggle. He said that he would not hurt me if I didn't scream. He released my neck and I took a huge breath. I didn't scream although I wanted to.

"He rolled me over onto my stomach and tied my hands behind me. Then he tied a blindfold over my eyes and told me not to try to look at him.

"He had tied my hands so tightly that I cried; he then loosened the knots slightly. He apologized. I asked him if he was going to kill me; I was shaking so much. He said no if I did everything he told me to do.

"He took a knife and sliced off my nightgown and underwear. I cried and said please don't hurt me. He started to touch me down there. I said please don't, and he stopped. I asked through tears why he was doing this to me. He just laughed. I knew he was going to rape me and kill me; I just knew it. I could not stop crying. He punched me a few times and told me to shut up. I shut up, Detective.

"He helped me to sit up on the bed. He said that he would be back and not to move. When he returned, he had something in his hand that touched my arm. I thought it was a gun. I started to cry again and cried to him that I knew he was going to shoot me. He said to shut up.

"He said he wanted me to be in a certain position, so he had me lie on my stomach with my head on my pillow and up on my knees. Suddenly, even though I was blindfolded, I could see flashes of light. I knew then that he was taking pictures, gross pictures. I am so ashamed."

"Linda, it's not your fault."

"It is. I should have let my fiancé move in like he wanted."

"Linda, it's not your fault. Please go on. You are doing a great job. I know this isn't easy for you."

"One time when he was putting me in obscene positions, his body touched mine. He was completely naked! He rubbed his thing against my back. I knew for sure then that he was going to rape me. He took picture after picture."

"Linda, did you say that he touched you with his penis?

It's important so that area described can be tested," Alissa said.

"I think that area has already been washed."

"Okay, please continue, Linda."

"Suddenly he left me again and when he returned to the bedroom, he told me to start counting slowly out loud to five hundred. If I did not, he would kill me.

"I started to count, crying all the time; I didn't hear any noise and stopped at fifty. When I did, he said keep counting or else.

"Finally, at about two hundred or so, I stopped. He was gone. I struggled to untie my hands. I realized that I could have gotten loose when he was there, but I know that he would have killed me if I did. I got the blindfold off; put on the first thing I could reach and ran to David's house. The rest you know.

"I am so thankful he did not rape me. What did he want?"

"I guess he just wanted pictures of a helpless and scared woman to satisfy his perverted mind. Thank you, Linda. Again, I know how hard this was for you. This will help us to catch him. Thank you."

"I hope you do. I am moving out today to my boyfriend's apartment."

"We will need to stay in touch with you, Linda, so please don't leave the area without letting us know where we can reach you."

"I will."

"One last thing, Linda, we need to accompany you back to the cottage to ask you to see if any of your private things have been taken by him, even if what he has taken is personal, private, and maybe embarrassing."

"Okay, if it is with you and you only."

At that point, Alissa shut off the recorder and said, "We then went to the cottage. The dresser drawers had been dusted by Forensics. Linda took her time looking. She thinks several articles of her underwear and bras were taken. She's not sure how many along are missing along with a personal item. She doesn't think any other things were taken."

"I so regret what a citizen had to go through. She is lucky," I said with some bitterness at our failure to catch him before he harmed this young woman.

"This guy is really creepy," Ray added.

"I fear it is only going to get worse. We have got to stop him."

Chapter Seventeen

The next morning, Alissa came to my office with an announcement.

"I've just gotten off the line with Linda Savage. Do you remember that I had asked her in the interview if she had noticed anything unusual about the intruder's voice or speech?"

"Hmm, remind me."

"Well, she was lying in bed last night and recalled that he told her not to try to escape, but he didn't say that; he said, 'don't try to 'excape' or I will kill you.' Get it, Chief?"

"Many people mispronounce that word, Alissa, how does that help us?"

"It may help us because she remembered hearing that word just recently. Linda had a handyman come to her home to replace some rotted wood on her patio deck. When she and I went to her house to determine what had been stolen, she gave me the guy's business card. Look!"

Harry D. West, Skilled Odd Jobber
"No job too small"
43 Lake Drive Circle, NW

"Anyway, while he was there, they talked about the jail-break in Grover City. It was then he said the convicts escaped through an old steam tunnel, except he didn't say escaped!"

"What did he say?"

"He said 'excaped' not escaped."

"Is Linda certain about this? She was terribly traumatized that evening. I'm sure that wouldn't hold up in court."

'Well, obviously that is possible, but Linda seems sure she heard him correctly. I would like to bring him in for an interview."

"I don't believe that the DA can build a case around that. Many people say 'escape' that way. Do we know anything about this handyman?"

"I haven't had a chance to look him up, yet."

"Alissa, we can't haul him in for an interview just because he mispronounces a word."

"I know, Chief, maybe we could ask Linda if she is willing to have him come back to her house."

"What?"

"Okay, forget it. It's a bad idea."

"It is a terrible idea; we couldn't ask her to do that. The best that I can suggest is that we put a watch on him for the next few days."

"All right, Chief. I hoped this would be the break we needed."

"One will come. Guys like our intruder always slip up. We'll have to wait for it. In the meantime, let's…"

At that moment, my phone rang.

"Good morning, Chief, is Alissa with you?"

"She is, what's up?"

"She left me a message about a handyman and Linda

Savage. I want to follow-up on it."

"Ray, she and I have just been through that. Why?"

"I checked this guy's record. He's had a few moral charges against him. He tried to fondle a woman in her home while he was 'handy-manning' a project for her."

"Hang on, Ray; Alissa, Ray says this guy has a record. I'll back off my position.

"Go get a search warrant and then bring him in for a little talk. Ray, Alissa is coming to see you."

"Alissa, ensure the warrant allows us to search for women's undergarments, computers, and photographs; we need to see what he does on social media."

"Got it. We will catch up later."

The next day, Harry West was asked to come to the police station.

"Mister West, I'm Detective Brown and this is Detective Riley. We've asked you to talk with us today about some break-ins in the Glendale area. You are not under arrest; you can leave anytime. We are recording this interview."

"Why talk to me? I don't know anything about them."

"Your name has come up recently, and we wanted to have your input."

"My input? What the hell are you talking about?"

"Someone has identified you as the person who assaulted them two nights ago."

"I didn't get into a fight with anyone."

"No, this involves forcibly holding someone against their will and terrorizing them into doing certain acts."

"That wouldn't be me. I don't do things like that."

"Look, Harry, we know about your past. You were found guilty of attempted rape; you served six years for it."

"Does that ring a bell with you?" Alissa asked.

"Okay, okay, but I didn't have anything to do with the one up in the Northeast section."

"What 'one up in the Northeast section' are you talking about?"

"You know, the one a few nights ago. Word gets around, you know."

"No, tell me."

"I heard some woman got herself tied up by her boyfriend after a fight. That's all I know."

"Where did you hear that?"

"Last night in Mickey's Bar on Seventh Street, some guy was telling how he and his girlfriend had a fight and he had to tie her up to shut her up."

"What is this guy's name?"

"I don't know; he's some twerp I've seen there before but he's not a regular."

"Can you describe him?"

"Well, you know Mickey keeps the lights down low, so it's hard to get a good look. He is a tall guy, about six feet, with brown or possibly reddish hair, has a beard, wears cowboy boots that make loud clicks when he walks."

"Anything else about him?"

"Yeah, he is strong. I saw him pick up a guy once and throw him to the ground."

"Didn't Mickey call us?"

"It was out in the parking lot and I was pretty drunk, so maybe I'm not sure it happened."

"You're lying, Harry. What happened?"

"I swear; I may be wrong about it even happening."

"You're holding back, Harry."

"Are you accusing me of the Savage thing?"

Ray and Alissa passed a look to each other. Savage's name had not been released to the public.

"We want to know what you know about it, that's all, Harry."

"I don't know anything."

"Harry, we have been searching your house while we speak. Several things have been reported as a result of that."

"What the hell? Am I being accused?"

"No, but we need to eliminate you as a suspect. As I said before, someone did identify you."

"Maybe I should have a lawyer."

"That's your right. Do you still want to talk to us?"

"I've got nothing to hide; I didn't do anything to anyone."

"Harry, we have your fingerprints at several of the homes which have been burglarized and at the woman's home who was attacked."

"You'll probably find my prints in many homes in the District. I make my living doing odd jobs for people. So what?"

"There are other things, Harry. We have found photographs in your cottage. We have photos of you and a woman both nude. There are several different women with their hands tied behind their backs. They are also blindfolded."

"What can you tell us about that?"

"Oh, those, yeah, some old girlfriends who were into that stuff."

"You photographed them in some really embarrassing positions. They don't look amused."

"Well, you know. Different strokes for different folks."

"Also, you seem to be a collector of underwear, women's underwear. Why is that?"

"I told you, already. Old girlfriends left things behind. I never know when they are coming back for more fun, so I didn't throw them out."

"Harry, we need the names of these women."

"I can't give you their names. Some of them have husbands. I can't do that to them."

"But you could tie them up and make them pose in compromising positions and take their pictures. I want those names now. Write them down. We will check them out," Ray said angrily.

"I want my name left out of this; give me a pen."

"No promises, Harry."

With that demand, West wrote down five names, three of which were from the Glendale Lake area.

"It looks like some of them were your neighbors. Were

151

you black mailing them?"

"Of course not! What do you think I am?"

"I'm not answering that, Harry. You need to answer that for yourself."

"I am not a criminal, if that's what you believe."

"Well, how can you afford the cottage and all the expenses which are part of living in Glendale? It seems too ritzy for you."

"I work. I work hard at my business."

"Your business lets you enter many homes in the area, does it not?"

"It does, but only when I am invited. Those in the pictures were just lonely and I was there. You know, a handyman."

"The recent break-in of a Glendale residence is very serious. Your penchant for tying up women and photographing them leaves us no choice, but to assume you might be involved."

"I'm not involved."

"Tell us what we will find on your computer. Our forensics people are looking at it now."

"I'm a single man, Detective. I like to check out the internet."

"What does that mean?"

"Alright, I go to porn sites. I look at women, no kids though, I mean it."

"Your story is very flimsy, Harry. Right now, I think you did it and the other break-ins."

"I did not."

"Prove it. Will you take a polygraph test?"

"I will, if it means you will leave me alone."

"One last request, Harry," Ray said, "We want you to be in a line-up and say a few words; will you do that?"

"I am beginning to think I need a lawyer."

"That's your right. Are you finished talking to us?"

"Look, several years ago, I did some bad things to a woman. I did my time, but this time I am innocent. I swear. I'll do what you ask. I'm innocent. After I got out of jail, I went straight. I haven't broken any laws since. I got married, but it didn't last. So I found other ways, legally, to get my kicks. You have to believe me. Yes, I diddled with a few neighbors, but they wanted it, I swear."

"Okay, Harry, let's do the lineup."

With that, Alissa went off to schedule a polygraph for that afternoon and arrange for a line-up.

Linda Savage was nervous, only begrudgingly willing to face her kidnapper in a lineup. Two police officers in plain clothes and four prisoners from the lockup, along with Harry West were asked to say, "If you try to escape, I will kill you."

When West said the word "escaped" properly, Linda nearly fainted; she had been mistaken.

"You were great, Linda, a real soldier. Thank you."

That afternoon, Harry West was wired up for the polygraph test. Ray told him he failed; it was a lie. The hope was it would convince him to confess to the break-ins, and the kidnapping and torture of Linda Savage.

West steadfastly refused to admit his guilt and was released. As he left the station, he told Ray that he would be getting a lawyer, so any further questions we could take up with his lawyer.

When Ray and Alissa told me of the results, I was crestfallen. I ordered them to provide constant surveillance of the area. I was determined he would not get away.

One last task was to contact the five women in the photographs. Each confessed embarrassment of their behavior, but none accused West of coercion or force. They had participated willingly. Two were married and asked that they not be identified. Their wishes were granted.

Harry wasn't off our radar, though. We would watch him closely, but we weren't sure his activities would present us with enough probable cause for an arrest.

The "evidence" we had did not prove his involvement with the break-ins or the attack. We would have to wait for him to make a mistake.

Chapter Eighteen

"Rob, what's troubling you? Can't sleep?"

"I can't, Anne. I lay awake thinking about the pervert out there. We thought we had him, but the only evidence we have is circumstantial. For now, we've had to let him walk away."

"It's not like you to fret over a case. You have a fine team of detectives; I'm sure they will find him."

"Maybe, maybe. In the meantime, he's free to hurt someone."

"Rob, I know you well enough after all these years of marriage. That isn't what's bothering you, is it?"

"No, Anne, it isn't. I have been agonizing about what you said to me a while back concerning your missing underwear. That kind of stuff is at the heart of this case. The pervert collects women's clothing."

"I regret saying anything to you about it, but it is true. Somehow, several things went missing. At first, I thought it was my scatterbrain, but it wasn't. Now, I am sure they went missing."

"So, you think it was Roy who stole them?"

"I don't want to believe that. I don't know what to think. He is such a nice guy and he is important in your life, our lives."

"Yeah, Anne, that's what makes this so tough for me to deal with. He's been like a father to me."

"Rob, I am going to tell you something that I should have done before. I don't want to now, but…"

"What is it?"

"On one of my trips to visit my family, I stopped at your mom's. We had a long talk about you, about Roy, about other things. I don't know exactly how to tell you what she said."

"Tell me what?"

"Okay, here goes. You remember that your mom and Roy were quite close at one time. Well, the move to Bards Crossing wasn't just because Mom wanted to get away from the welfare situation. It was coincidental that her courses were finished and she was hired at her job in Bards Crossing, but her main reason for leaving was to break off the relationship with Roy."

"What? Are you kidding me?"

"You see, Rob. She and Roy had been lovers for a few years. She said that she loved Roy. He was very kind to you and to her, but he had certain ways about him, which made her feel unsafe. And there were other things she wouldn't accept."

"Roy? The kindest guy in the world?"

"He is, and Mom agrees that he is a special person whom she still has feelings for. It's just that…"

"Come on, Anne, just tell me what the problem is."

"Okay, promise that you will not get angry."

"Come on, Anne."

"I mean it, Rob, promise me."

"Okay, I won't, Anne, I won't get angry with you, Mom, or Roy. I promise."

"Okay, Rob. Mom didn't go into all the details, but she said that Roy liked to tie her hands behind her back when they were…"

"What? That…"

"You promised, Rob. She said that he was always gentle with her and never hurt her. The things that made her realize she had to break away from him was his desire to take photos of her naked."

"That son-of-a-bitch!"

"Rob, you need to listen, not go off half-cocked."

"Okay, what else?"

"She asked him to destroy any photos and he said he did. The other thing that bothered her was finding him fondling some of her underclothes. At that point, she decided to get you and her out of Augusta."

"Why didn't Mom ever say anything to me?"

"Rob, Sweetheart, these are very personal things that a woman can say to another woman, but not to a man, especially her son. You can understand that."

"I guess I do, Anne. What you've told me, I would not have ever suspected about Roy."

"I know, Rob, it is painful to say."

"If it were anybody else telling me this about Roy, I would deck them. It is an eye-opener, though."

"Rob, Mom asked me never to tell you unless it was critical, but I believe you need to know. It may make things easier for you to do your job. God forbid that Roy is responsible for these break-ins."

"Oh, God, Anne. It breaks my heart to hear those things happened to my mom."

"Mom does not have bad feelings about Roy. He was good to you; he was good to her in most ways. Roy just wasn't what she wanted in a husband or lover. I think she still has feelings for him."

"You know, Anne, I will never understand women. I love you and Mom. What you have said will not affect what I think about Mom, but about Roy I'm not so sure. He mistreated my mother and yet she says she still has some feelings for him."

"I can't understand that, Anne."

"I know, Rob, it's that way with women sometimes."

"He isn't a bad man. In my heart, he is still my father."

"That's good, Rob. I'm sorry I had to say these things."

"Anne, do you honestly believe that Roy stole your underclothes?"

"As I said before, I don't know for certain. I do know that some of my things are missing."

"It's just so hard to believe that he would do that. Worse, is what Mom said about him."

"I know. I'm sorry. Can you accept some advice, Rob?"

"Maybe."

"I suggest that you put this in the back of your mind. Try to not let it affect what goes on at work."

"I don't know if I'm able to do that."

"Look! Roy is not the first man to want to play out these kinds of things during sex, and not the last. That he did at one time, does not make him guilty of what's going on today. He is your friend! You need to remember that."

"I know, but when I think about him and Mom, I'd like to punch him out."

"I expect you to keep your promise, Rob."

"I will, Anne. Should I ever tell Mom that you've told me these things?"

"Never. Keep it between us. Even though she gave me permission, it's much better that way."

"Well. I've wanted to talk with Roy about other things in his past, but I haven't had the nerve to do it. Maybe this will give me the courage to do it."

"You should, if it will put things between you to rest. No violence, Rob."

"No, I promise."

"We haven't had him over for here some time. Why not invite him around for dinner?"

"Maybe that's a good idea, Anne, but I think our conversation would go easier if just the two of us talk. He certainly cares for you, but I'm afraid he wouldn't open up about things with you present. My questions will be too sensitive."

"Do you think that what's bothering you is more on your plate than his?"

"What do you mean?"

"What I'm saying is this. You may be making too much of the things, which are not that important."

"It could be, Anne, but my gut tells me they are

159

important."

During our years together, I had not told Anne about the strange coincidences which had occurred in Roy's life, nor would I tell her tonight. Roy's possible involvement in the deaths of John Goldie's murderer, and the acid blinding of his first wife's killer needed answers. Roy's interests in being a lock smith, his elation over Heidi's murderer's death, were all things I needed to have Roy explain.

"I have an idea, Rob. Tomorrow is Friday, why don't you invite him over? I will leave in the afternoon to visit my mother. She's been inviting me and I have put it off. It's the right time for me to do it."

"I hate to ask you to leave. I believe it would help, though."

"Anything for you, Sweetheart."

"I am nervous about asking possibly embarrassing questions about his past."

"So, don't ask him; play the reminiscences game; you know, talk about times you shared together. Say things like, 'Remember when…,' that may bring out what you need to know."

"I guess it's worth a try, Anne."

"Come on, Rob, don't waver on this. Get it done. It will be good for both of you."

"Okay, thank you, Anne, goodnight."

Perhaps she was right. Sleep did not come easily and I lay awake turning over thoughts about my mother, which Anne had shared. I was now forced to judge Roy in a different light.

Before tonight's eye-opening conversation, Roy was a teacher, an unblemished teacher, of all that was good, and right for me and my mother. Now, he was exposed. He is a good person, but not without faults. Faults, which I hoped would not lead me to arrest him, and worse, destroy the one man in this world who treated me as his son.

Chapter Nineteen

In the morning, I called Roy and he accepted my invitation to a dinner of ribeye steaks and potatoes on the grill. In anticipation of this evening, the rest of the workday dragged by. In a way, I looked forward to our talking about the past; in another, I dreaded it.

Early in the evening, the doorbell rang and Roy began with his usual flair.

"Evening, Master Robbie; thank you for the invite. I tire of cooking for myself."

"Come in, come in. Anne had to visit her mother, so I guess that you will have to put up with me."

"Well, I should go then; another boring evening with you is too much," he said with his usual, 'I'm kidding smile.' "

"As I remember, you're not much fun either," I said in return.

Moving to the patio, I cracked open beers and we began to chitchat.

"What's been keeping you so busy lately, Roy? You haven't dropped by in a while."

"I've been seeing a cute thing from the City who is taking up a lot of my time."

"Really! That's good to hear. We've been a bit worried about you."

"It isn't very serious, although she thinks it is. I'm just tagging her for a while until the fun wears off."

"That doesn't sound like you, Roy. You and Heidi had

something special for many years."

"Yeah, that's true, but I don't see anyone special on the horizon at this point in my life, so I get my kicks wherever I can."

"You need to meet another Heidi."

"Probably, but I'm enjoying myself these days."

"I thought the world of Heidi, Roy, she had a warm heart along with being so beautiful."

"You want to know something? She and I had a big chuckle the night after you came to spend the first summer with us. When you first met her, I thought your eyes were going to bug right out of your head."

"I know; I'm ashamed at what I thought about her at the time."

"Yeah, you didn't give it up for a while, either. Volunteering to do the laundry was a bit over the top. Heidi didn't want you pawing over her underwear with her cycles and all."

"Now, I'm really embarrassed, Roy."

"Don't be; you were well into puberty at that time; you weren't thinking with the right head. By the time you arrived for the last summer with us, Heidi said that you were getting a steady diet of it somewhere, so you no longer ogled her."

"Roy, I never ogled your wife, please."

"Well, when I had to be away for a day, she could feel your eyes on her. I think today you can appreciate that. She said that she wasn't threatened by you; it was just that she didn't want her warmth toward you to be taken wrong."

"Roy, I never…"

"Relax, Robbie, you were a kid; I trusted you, but I trusted Heidi more, so let it go."

"Roy, Heidi told me one time during the last summer I worked on the farm, that your 'inheritance' was not quite a true story. She didn't say why, but it stuck in my mind."

"Heidi, bless her little heart, sometimes said things that weren't quite on track. I tried to have her understand that thinking something doesn't necessarily make it so. I'm not sure that she ever took that to heart."

"Well, Roy, in my eyes she was the best."

"She was, Robbie, she was. After Heidi was murdered, I really went into a funk. I couldn't let go of the idea that some bastard had hurt her in the way he had. I felt I had to make it right for her."

"What do you mean, Roy?"

"I mean I had to make sure that whoever did it was punished."

"Well, the Portland PD had the guy nailed and he got killed."

"I know; it brought great happiness to me. He was not going to get away."

"But he never went to trial, Roy. He was never found guilty."

"True, Robbie, but the justice system is too slow. Even if he had been tried and found guilty, it would have taken twenty years or more to put him in the ground. That's not justice."

"I understand, Roy, but it is our system."

"Too bad. Someone fixed the system. I have no regrets about that."

"But Roy, it's wrong. That kind of justice leads to anarchy. We need to let the law deal out the appropriate punishment. You need to believe in that."

"I don't have much to believe in anymore, except the…"

"Roy, you can build a new life; you can afford to go traveling; take boat cruises; go anywhere you want; find another woman. Doesn't that appeal to you?"

"You know, Robbie, I've been on a number of cruises. Besides getting drunk and screwing a lot of lonely women, there isn't much to write home about. I like to stay around here and observe things going on."

"Did you ever get your locksmith business going?"

"Why do you ask, Robbie? Is that a problem for you?"

"No, but…"

"It was never going to be a business; I think I told you it was only for my pleasure."

"Well, yeah, you did. What kind of pleasure does it give you?"

"Oh, I don't really know. Power, maybe, whatever that means."

"I see. What do you do to occupy your time these days?"

"My doctor has told me to get out and walk more, so I like to hike around the Lake a few times a week. For another, Robbie, I heard through the grapevine that your department is in a world of hurt. Have you been able to catch the burglar, yet?"

"You know I can't talk about ongoing cases, Roy, even though I would like to tell you."

"You want to know what I think?"

At that moment, I needed to flip the steaks. It gave me time to think of a weak, silly response.

"What do you think?"

"I believe that the guy is local. Someone who has time on his hands. Someone who doesn't have a woman to keep tabs on his activities. He has time to scout his victims without their knowledge."

"Why do you think that, Roy?"

"You know, maybe they undress with the light on and the curtains open. So, maybe it entices the guy."

"Yes, Roy, I can see that."

"Maybe they are careless about locking their doors. That sort of thing."

"I guess we figured that may be true. How do you think he gains entrance to the cottages?"

"Easy, Robbie, even after your flyers went out, neighbors tell me that they often forget to lock up. You know, that area has felt safe for years. New people aren't frightened, so it makes no problem for this guy."

"That's helpful, Roy. I'll tell my detectives to warn them better."

"That may help, but I doubt it."

"Why do you say that?"

"Because whoever is doing this knows how to get in."

"That's discouraging, Roy. Do you have any idea how we can get the residents to be more careful?"

"I don't, Robbie. The women around here are air-heads; they don't seem to care about their safety; maybe they are asking for it, but it serves them right."

"Roy, I can't believe you said that."

"In truth, Robbie, getting people to take responsibility is a monumental job, I'm afraid. You must know that?"

"You're probably right, Roy. In your travels, do you know of anyone who is a fence for stolen property?"

"A fence? Who's going to fence underwear, Robbie?"

At that point, my heart sank. We had not released that information to the public.

"How do you know it's underwear he steals?"

"The girl I told you about, told me. She heard it from a friend of a friend who lives in Glendale."

"Do you know who that is?"

"No, I'll ask her the next time I see her."

"Okay, Roy, great, the sooner the better. Better yet, why don't you give me her name? I can check it out for myself."

"I'd better okay it with her first. She is after all 'my love.'"

After dinner was done, Roy and I drank some more, and smoked cigars that Roy had brought.

"Way back when, Roy, you told me about the guy who shot your first wife. How was he not able to see anymore?"

"Someone threw acid in his face, which the son-of-a-bitch deserved."

"Did the police have any idea who did it?"

At that, Roy just smiled and said, "Sometimes life just balances out."

"I remember poor John Goldie that summer. Didn't his accused killer get whacked somehow, Roy?"

"Yeah, again some do-gooder took a bat to his head and put him out of his misery, and ours." Again, the smile.

As the evening morphed to night, Roy and I said our good-byes. I had my answers; they were circumstantial, but they clearly put Roy in a bad light. I knew this would not turn out well for him or me.

Chapter Twenty

Several weeks later, a frantic call was made to the 911 dispatchers. A friend of a Glendale District resident pleaded for police to send an ambulance to the home of Miss Abigail Stevens at 35 Lake Drive Southeast.

Upon arrival, Officer Holly quickly secured the crime scene. When Alissa arrived, Linda Holly gave to her a brief report.

The friend, Mrs. Patricia White, and Miss Stevens had planned to go shopping that morning. When Miss Stevens did not respond to a knock on her door, Mrs. White tried the door and found it unlocked. She entered the home and found Miss Stevens. She was completely naked with tape over her mouth and her hands bound behind her back. Her legs were also trussed with tie-wraps. A blindfold covered her eyes.

Panicking, Mrs. White called 911. She was told to remove the tape, remove the blindfold, untie the woman, and to remain on the line until police arrived. It had taken many minutes for Patricia White to find a pair of scissors to cut the arm and leg shackles to free the moaning Miss Stevens before the medics arrived.

Since Miss Stevens was alive, the dispatcher's instructions were correct, but they did compromise the crime scene, much to the dismay of Officer Holly.

Alissa could see that Abigail Stevens had been severely beaten. She had bruises over extensive parts of her body. Her wrists had been bound so tightly that deep red indentations encircled her arms. Evidence of attempted strangulation was evident around the woman's neck.

The ambulance medics found a weak pulse. Abigail Stevens was close to death. She was rushed to the Augusta Hospital ICU where doctors struggled to save her life. The admitting physician was certain that she had been sexually assaulted, so a rape kit was administered in accordance with police procedure.

The trauma was so severe that Miss Stevens was not physically or emotionally ready for an interview until a week later when Alissa visited her in the hospital. Even after that, Abigail could not relate what happened without uncontrollable sobbing.

When the interview was complete, Alissa returned to the station to update us with the heartrending recording.

"Abigail, I am Detective Riley from the Augusta Police. We are actively searching for the man who did this to you. I need to ask you some questions. Are you willing to do this?"

"I'm not sure. There are many things that I wish I could block out. There are things I don't want to remember."

"Anything you can remember will help us. Do you mind if I record our discussion?"

"Okay, I will try."

"Abigail, can you tell me what happened that night?"

"I remember I got ready for bed. My usual time is nine-thirty. Sometime after I was in bed, the man jumped on me. He had his hands around my throat, choking me.

"He stopped before I blacked out. He rolled me on my stomach and tied my hands behind my back. He told me if I screamed he would shoot me. I promised I wouldn't.

"He told me to keep my head down while he blindfolded me. I said I would. Then he cut off my nightgown and underwear. He began to take pictures."

"Abigail, how could you tell that?"

"The blindfold was something he must have found in my dresser. It was not that good as a blindfold. I could actually see if I looked down so I could see flashes."

"What happened next?"

At that point, Abigail broke into sobs. Alissa hugged her and waited. Abigail continued.

"He must have made sure the blinds were closed because I could see that he had my small bedside lamp on. Then he began to make me pose in disgusting positions. I could see more flashes. He's sick, Detective."

"He is, Abigail. Is there anything unusual about him you remember?"

"He is strong; his hands felt like iron; his voice was deep and he spoke slowly."

"What happened next?"

"He did what he came to do; he raped me; he raped me over and over. When I started to scream, he began punching me. Then he put tape over my mouth. At first, he covered my mouth and nose. I panicked and couldn't breathe. I thrashed about until he took the tape away from my nose. Then I must have blacked out. After that,

Detective, I don't remember anything. If Patricia hadn't found me, I would have died."

"He must have panicked. He beat you unmercifully. We think he tried to strangle you again. You are lucky, Abigail."

"Lucky? Lucky? You think to be raped over and over again in my own room, in my own bed is lucky?"

"I'm sorry, Abigail, poor choice of words; I only meant that you are alive."

"I'm alive physically, Detective, but I am emotionally dead. My life will never be the same. I will never trust a man again. Lucky?"

"I'm so sorry, Abigail. We will catch him and put him in jail for the rest of his life."

"I'm sorry, Detective, you cannot promise that. If you do catch him, some soft-headed judge will let him off with a few years. That's not justice and my life is ruined."

"We'll catch him; I promise, Abigail."

"Well, you do that. Do you know that my boyfriend came to the hospital two days ago and told me he never wanted to see me again? He said I must have wanted it, a party gone bad."

"I am sorry, Abigail. I wish there was something I could do."

"There is nothing you can do except to get this bastard."

"I will go now. If you need anything, please call me. I will check on you, if you would like."

"Thank you, Detective, but you can do nothing for me.

172

If you do catch him, I will have to face him in court and I will not do that! I will be forced to relive every moment I can remember and some lawyer will grill me as though I wanted this hell visited on me. The justice system can go to hell!"

Alissa turned off the recording. The room was quiet.

"I want this guy caught, now!" I nearly yelled.

"We are doing all we can, Chief. This guy knows the system. He leaves us no clues or evidence of himself. Abigail was raped, probably more than once as she says, but no semen evidence was found, nothing to connect a suspect. No unidentified fingerprints, nothing," Ray said exasperated.

"I suggest we go back to West and haul him in," Alissa proposed. "I want to get a confession from him; he is guilty as sin."

"Okay, let's try him again," I agreed.

Harry West was brought to the station by Ray. His demeanor was defiant.

"Where were you last Friday night?"

"I was home watching television."

"Can anyone verify that?"

"No, you know I live alone. Who would be there to say I was home, Smartass?"

"Look, Harry, we know you are hurting these women. You need to tell us, now."

"I will never confess to something I didn't do. I'm leaving; you have nothing on me."

"You're not going anywhere until you confess."

"I want a lawyer."

"Are you still willing to talk to us?"

"No, I want a lawyer, now."

At this point, West was read his Miranda rights.

"Okay, Harry. I am arresting you. The charges will be suspicion of breaking and entering in the night time with intent to steal. Three charges of causing bodily harm to three females, a charge in the rape of one female, and finally, two charges of assault and battery of two females will be filed."

"Charge whatever you want; I will be out tomorrow."

The District Attorney, Michael Smith, was given a full brief of the charges.

"Chief, your case is entirely circumstantial. In fact, it is so weak I am surprised you can't see that. I have nothing to take to a Grand Jury," DA Smith said.

Harry West was right; we released him the next morning. It was an embarrassing day.

We would have to play a waiting game for the next attack. We had done all we could do to prevent another assault, but it was not enough. The citizens of Glendale District knew that they needed to be on alert, but would they take precautions?

Worse, thoughts of my friend, Roy, kept looming up in my mind. I knew that Tara Kimble's cottage was next to Roy's, and Abigail's was two doors away.

I thought to myself, "Roy, if it is you, you can't be that

stupid. Please, God, don't let it be Roy!"

It was clear to me that it wouldn't be long before Alissa and Ray would start to pose questions about the odd guy who lives in the Southeast section.

Chapter Twenty-One

A week later my office phone rang.

"Chief, it's happened; what we feared," Ray blurted out.

"What's happened?"

"We just got a 911 call. A dog walker found a body on Lake Drive across the street from the cottage at 39 Southeast. Alissa and I are headed out there now."

"Okay, Ray, stay in touch."

I quickly took out a Glendale map. Number 39 was the home of Douglas Burns. His cottage was located two doors from Abigail Stevens, and two doors from Rebecca Shaw in the other direction. Had we missed something in our interviews of residents?

I decided to drive out to Lake Drive and see for myself.

"What have we got here?"

"A dead woman, white, wrapped up in clear plastic. Hands bound, tape over her mouth, that's about it until Doctor March releases the body to the morgue and schedules a post-mortem," Ray offered.

"We've cordoned off the area; our forensics team has arrived and begun their work," Alissa disclosed.

"Great! Any idea, who she is?"

"Not for certain, but a Jason Green was driving around Lake Drive Circle and stopped when he saw us. He has been frantically looking for his girlfriend, Jane Newman. He's over there by his car."

"Let's have a few words with him. After that, Alissa, take him over to the body. He may be able to identify her,"

I ordered.

Alissa asked Jason Green to follow her to the police car for an interview.

"Mister Green, I want to ask you a few questions. You said that you're looking for your girlfriend this morning. When did you realize that she was missing?"

"This morning; I came over to pick her up."

"Where does she live?"

"She lives in the cottage at number 27 in the Northeast section."

"Do you and Miss Newman live together?" Ray began his questioning.

"No, we are planning to be married next year; we decided that we would wait until then. We haven't told either of our parents, yet."

"Why is that?"

"Her parents don't believe that I am the right person for their daughter."

"Why is that?"

"I don't know; I guess I'm not from the same layer of crust that they are. He is a bigwig in banking; my folks are just average people. They probably think I'm fortune hunting or something, but I love Jane; I'm not after her money. I have a good job."

"I see. Why were you at her home this morning?"

"We were going to shop for an engagement ring and then let her parents know we were engaged. We weren't sure how the day would go after that."

"Where do they live?"

"They are in Biscayne, about three hundred miles from here; that's why we wanted to get started early and then drive out there to tell them."

"Okay, for now, Mister Green. I have an unpleasant question for you. Would you be willing to take a look at a young woman we've found?"

"I would if it will help you."

"Thanks, please follow Detective Riley."

Ray came over to me and said, "Chief, I noticed a cut on his right hand and a scratch on his face. I think we have to spend some time with him."

After a few minutes, a great cry came from the area where the body lay. Jason Green identified the woman as Jane Newman who lived at 27 Lake Drive NE.

"Okay, Ray, bring him in; get a crew out to Newman's cottage right away."

As tough as it was, we needed to further question him. I felt his showing up at this time was a bit too convenient. At the station, Ray and Alissa began.

"Mister Green, thank you for talking to us at this terrible time. You are not being detained; you are free to leave at any time, but it would help us to understand what happened last night."

"I'll do anything I can to help."

"What is your full name?"

"Jason Michael Green."

"Where do you live?"

"I live by myself at 2364 Twelve Oaks in the Whitfield section."

"Do you know of anyone who would do this to Jane?"

"I have no idea, Officer. She is sweet to everyone."

"Can you tell us whom she had for close friends?"

"She only had one best-friend. Her name is Sheila Dawson over in Buckland County."

"Do you have her address?"

"Sorry, I don't. She wasn't one of my favorite people."

"Why is that?"

"She was always cold to me. It was like she couldn't stand to have me around."

"But, she was Jane's best friend."

"Yes."

"When did you last see Jane?"

"Let's see; it must have been around nine-thirty last night."

"Where did you go when you left Jane?"

"I went home; watched the late show and went to bed."

"So, no one can verify that?"

"I'm afraid not. My roommate is away visiting on a trip."

"What's your roommate's name?"

"Michael Pitts."

"When you left, Jason, did she seem nervous or out of sorts in any way?"

"No, not that I noticed. She did say that with the break-ins and the young women who were raped, she was being extra careful about locking up at night. She was thinking about getting a German Shepherd for protection. I told her to call me immediately if anything frightened her. I'm only five miles away."

"So, your last evening with Jane was pleasant, nothing out of the ordinary?"

"Yes, we went out for dinner and went back to her cottage for a nightcap."

"Are you two intimate?"

"If you mean, do we have sex, yes."

"Okay. When did you last have sex?"

"Why is that important?"

"Because we think that she may have been raped. That means…"

"Oh, God, no."

"That means we could eliminate you."

"Well, it was two nights ago."

"Did you use a condom?"

"No, she's on the pill."

"Okay; did you have a fight that night?"

"No, why do you ask?"

"Well, Jason, we've noticed a couple of things. For one, how did you get that scratch on your face? I can see that it is healing, but…"

"Oh, that, we were horsing around that night and she accidently scratched me. She felt bad about it."

"And the cut on your hand?"

"Oh, that. I was opening a package and the knife slipped.

It bled quite a bit."

"Where did that happen?"

"At Jane's cottage, in the living room."

"Would you be willing to take a lie detector test?"

"Why, do you think I could have done this?"

"We ask everyone to do that."

"I don't know. I'm not familiar with this; am I a suspect? Do I need a lawyer?"

"I can give you the stock answer; everyone is a suspect. If you want a lawyer, you can have one. Are you still willing to work with us?"

"I guess so; I have nothing to hide."

"Okay, Jason, thank you. I will have one scheduled for tomorrow. We'll call you with the time and you can return to the station. We also need a cheek swab, a blood sample, and fingerprints; are you willing to give those?"

"Well, okay. If it helps to show you I'm innocent."

Concluding the interview, Alissa and Ray came to my office.

"Well, what do you think about Mister Green?"

"I'm not comfortable with him, Chief. I'm not saying that he is the one responsible for Newman's death, but the wounds he has and his lack of emotion about her death bothers me."

"Does he have an alibi?"

"Not one we can check out," Ray answered.

"There is something we can do, though. He gave us the name of Jane Newman's closest friend. I want to talk to her, Chief," Alissa said.

"Makes sense, Alissa. When will we be getting the post-mortem and search results of Newman's cottage?"

"Tomorrow for the post-mortem, and late tomorrow we'll have the polygraph of Green. The search of Newman's cottage will take another day," Ray replied.

"What about Green's apartment?"

"He's given us permission to search it."

"Good, let's get together again when we have results. Thanks for your hard work."

Chapter Twenty-Two

"Chief, we have the preliminary results of the post-mortem and the two search results," Ray said.

"I have the polygraph test results. Also, I have some news from my talk with Sheila Dawson, Jane's best friend," Alissa added.

"Give me the post-mortem highlights first, Ray"

"You know who the unfortunate woman was, Jane Newman: white, long blond hair, age 24. Death by strangulation, Doctor March can't say for certain if she was raped, but sperm was present. Swabs were taken and sent to the lab. Given the boyfriend's activities with her we won't know until the testing is complete."

"Getting a DNA result would be a great gift," I added.

"Since she was intimate with Green, the lab will have extra work. Let's hope. Doctor March isn't sure if we will be lucky there. As we observed when we found Jane, she had many contusions. March estimates they covered more than forty percent of her body. The beatings were vicious; this appears to be a crime of passion. Doctor March said that the indication of some of the contusions was strange, though."

"What was strange, Ray?"

"Well, he said that some of the bruises appear to have been inflicted well before the night she died because they appeared to be in the process of healing."

"What? If Jason is telling us the truth that he did not see her for the past few days, then Jane's killer is not Jason."

"Perhaps, his polygraph results will help to answer that, Chief, at least, I hope it will."

"So, someone has been torturing this poor woman for some time," I said with disgust, "How about the searches?"

"In Newman's cottage, the forensics team found spots of blood, but not any great amount. Perhaps, these were from Jane's nosebleed, but may prove to be from Green's 'knife accident.' The forensics lab will be comparing the samples to Newman's blood and Green's.

"Fingerprints are all over the house, hers obviously, and most likely, Green's. They did find three prints on the back door, which are possibly the index, middle, and ring fingers. They appear to be from a right hand," Ray explained.

"How is the search for a match going?"

"Right, Chief, IAFIS is still a slow search through millions of prints. I hope we get a break there."

"Yes, it may lead us to the burglar; though so far we haven't been able to identify any prints at those sites."

"Leaving fingerprints in Newman's house doesn't make sense if it's the same person. It's one thing to stage a panty raid and leave no prints by wearing gloves; then to kill Newman and be careless."

"Of course, you are correct, Alissa; it wouldn't make sense, but as we know, criminals are not the brightest lot in society."

"Another thing we find strange is that Newman's cottage was not torn up. No drawers were rifled; nothing looked to be otherwise disturbed."

"So, this didn't start out as a robbery that turned into a vicious, cold-blooded murder."

"No, Chief, I don't think so. Someone targeted her."

"What did we find at Green's apartment?"

"It's neat as a pin. The two roommates appear to be neat freaks. The roommate is away, so we had to call her."

"Her?"

"Yes, it's a her."

"Didn't you say the roommate's name is Michael Pitts?"

"We did," Alissa answered, "But her name is Michaela. Green says everybody calls her Michael."

"What? Are they lovers, Alissa? Was Green two-timing Jane?"

"According to Michaela, no. She's only been renting there for two months. She has a fiancé and is getting married in three months," Ray explained.

"Something more interesting about Jason Green came up in my conversation with Sheila Dawson," Alissa interrupted, "As I said, she is Jane's good friend. Sheila said that everything was not as rosy between Green and Jane as he wants us to believe."

"Sheila said that he had been pushing to move in with Jane at the cottage, but Jane's father had forbidden it. He owns the cottage and lets Jane live there rent free.

"Again, according to Sheila, Jane wanted to wait until marriage before they had sex, but Green forced himself on her one night. Jane threatened to call the police, but didn't."

"Why not? It was rape if this Sheila is not telling a tale," I declared.

"Sheila said that Jane was afraid he might be too good to let him get away. Maybe she wouldn't have another chance at marriage."

"That kind of thinking is totally stupid. There are many good men out there, if that is what she wanted," I said, raising my voice.

"It's worse than that. Sheila said that lately, Green has been hitting Jane. She told Jane to move in with her, but she refused."

"Well, Alissa, if Green has been hitting her, wouldn't those bruises on Jane look…"

"No, Chief, Doctor March says these bruises were made within the last two days of her life. They are just starting to heal."

"I just can't believe that a beautiful young woman could allow herself to be trapped into thinking that marriage at any cost is good for her," I interrupted.

"Well, Jane told Sheila she was thinking about breaking off the relationship. Sheila said that Jane was going to tell him this week that they were through."

"Chief, it's time we haul his ass back in for a tough interview," Ray said.

"Great thought, Ray, but we can't. He's lawyered up; his attorney called this morning. Green will not be talking to us again.

"I spoke to DA Smith. Unless we can find something

concrete to charge Green with, he is free to walk."

"We can keep an eye on him; can't we, Chief?"

"We must, but resources are getting thin. We're still spending bucks in Glendale to keep that under surveillance, so adding Buckland to the mix kills our budget. Sorry."

"That's life in this game. We'll keep you posted on the print search," Alissa added.

"One last thing, Chief, a neighbor of Newman said that they heard a car door slam sometime after two in the morning on the night before she was found. When she went to her living room window, she saw a dark colored Mercedes back out of the lover's lane across the street. It drove toward the Southeast section," Ray explained.

"How did she know it was a Mercedes?"

"Her husband was a Mercedes car buff; she attended car shows with him and keeps up to date on them."

"It's quite dark out that way. Is she sure?"

"Yes, it happens that there is a small street lamp located three doors away. The car drove past it, which helped."

"Did any patrol unit happen to spot it? We are supposed to be keeping a sharp eye on that area."

"I checked the logs to see if anything was reported, but there was not."

"Who was on duty at that time, Ray?"

"It was Corporal Linda Holly, Chief."

"I'll check on that when I get a chance, Ray."

Chapter Twenty-Three

An hour later my office phone rang. It was the familiar voice of my longtime friend, Abner, the big man who always spoke softly.

"Robbie, Abner here. I know I left you in a lurch awhile back. I can't say much more about the case we're working on, except that we are closer to making an arrest."

"That's good, Abner; I wish I could say the same about our problem out here."

"Oh, you mean the burglar?"

"Yes, it has become more serious, though. He has physically tortured and killed a woman. We have to get him before he does it again."

"Robbie, the reason for my call is that we have uncovered some information related to your area. I can't say where it came from; what I can tell you, is you have been chasing the wrong guy."

"How do you know about that, Abner? I thought the FBI chases national bandits."

"We have sources."

"You mean murderers and pimps like you had in Boston?"

"Robbie, easy, easy. Yes, we had a rogue agent there. He was caught and put in jail."

"Well, is your informant reliable, Abner?"

"I can't say anything further about the source."

"Well, why tell me anything then; it's no help at all."

"Robbie, as an old friend, I can only say that you may

want to look a little closer at people you would never suspect. I'm not saying who. You probably can guess whom I mean. This person has been very close to you."

"Are you serious, Abner? I cannot believe that! I can't. I won't believe that!"

"My informant says your person is not connected to my case, but this person is involved with your case."

"What have you been told, Abner?"

"Again, I can't do that. To tell you would compromise my source, I'm sorry to say."

"Abner, we're friends; you know you can trust me; tell me."

"I'm afraid I can't do that, old friend. I spoke to the Section Chief about this specifically, and he absolutely forbids it. He did say I could give you this oblique warning, that's all."

"Abner, do you realize what you are doing to me? I'm not going to start doubting my friends, including you."

"I can appreciate that. I'm sorry, Robbie. That's all I can say."

"How do you know your informant is not just making this up?"

"The person has been very reliable in the past. I have no reason to doubt."

"Your informant is wrong, Abner."

"My informant has been exhaustively vetted. I can only advise you, Robbie; you must make your own decisions. Good luck, old friend."

"I don't like it, Abner, but I understand your situation. I just can't accept that."

With that, the call with Abner was over.

In light of what Ray had told me earlier, I then called Captain William Weeks of the Patrol Unit to come to my office.

"Bill, I have something I need to discuss with you."

"Yes, Chief, what's the problem?"

"I have learned that on the night of the Linda Savage assault, Corporal Linda Holly was on duty in the Glendale District; she reported a Mercedes C-Class Coupe in one of the wooded parking spots along the Circle. In fact, it was nearly across the road from Savage's cottage."

"Yes, she spoke to me about it after the assault was reported. She was in another area at the time. She was first on the scene."

"Bill, she spotted a black Mercedes parked without any occupants, no parkers getting their thrills. That is very suspicious; can you tell me why she didn't record the tag number or call it in?"

"Linda is a good officer, Chief. She didn't call in a request for identification because there was another call for her to answer."

"It's a blatant disregard of responsibility, Bill. An unoccupied car in the area where we have placed a focus to apprehend a burglar and rapist, and she didn't think enough about it to find out who owns it? There were units who could have answered the other call."

"I will talk to her, Chief."

"See that you do. A note in her personnel jacket is called for."

"Chief, she made a mistake; Linda is one of our best officers."

"We may have been able to catch this guy if she hadn't messed up. I want you to ensure that any patrol officer who finds similar circumstances anywhere in the City to ID the owner."

"That's my policy, Chief, she screwed up."

"Bill, fix it. We have a new Police Commissioner who is starting to put pressure on us. Believe me, I understand, Bill, but we can't let these kinds of slip-ups happen."

"I will reprimand her and make a formal report of duty issues."

"Okay, Bill, just talk to her. Let her know that I am behind her, but no more mistakes."

Backing down a bit in personnel matters is one of my shortcomings on the job, but I didn't want to ruin an officer's career.

"Alright, Chief, I'll get it done. All patrol units will be notified."

"Also, talk to Ray Brown; I want a DMV report of Mercedes C-Class Coupes registered in Augusta. There shouldn't be that many, I hope."

After Captain Weeks left, I sat in my office overwhelmed with thoughts that I did not want to consider. I already knew Roy owned a Mercedes of that model, but I was stubbornly refusing to let it rent any space in my head.

A day later, Ray had the automobile report and more.

"Chief, the only person in Glendale with a Mercedes C-Class Coupe is a guy named Roy Hepburn who lives at 31 Lake Drive Southeast. There are three others in Augusta and four in Portland, but that's not all," Ray said.

"What do you mean 'that's not all?' "

"I mean that this is our big break in the murder of Jane Newman."

"How is that?"

"I'll tell you; we are excited; we matched the prints found on Newman's door. You'll never guess who they belong to."

"I can see you're excited, Ray, but I'm not up for games. Whose are they?"

"This guy, Roy Hepburn, who also owns the Mercedes."

The pain of what Ray said could not have been worse than if Ray had stabbed me with a knife.

"Oh, no, not Roy," I cried to myself, "It can't be you, Roy."

"There's no mistake, Ray?"

"No, Chief, his prints are on file because he applied for a concealed carry permit a couple of years ago. We fingerprinted him."

"Why did it take this long to match them?"

"Because we were checking fingerprints of criminals, not CCW applicants."

"I see; maybe we need to change our process for the

future. What do you plan to do about Hepburn, Ray?"

"We need to bring him in today, Chief. I think we need to push full force on this guy since we have all agreed that the intruder most likely lives in Glendale."

"I agree," I responded with great reluctance, "We must talk to him. Prepare to obtain search warrants for his car and home."

I felt I now had to consider my friend as a suspect. Maybe Abner's canary was right; Roy was involved in this heinous crime. It was the hardest thing I ever had to face.

I called the four detectives together and gave them the information Abner had implied, but without the details.

"Even though this tip came from an unnamed source, we have to take it seriously," I reluctantly ordered, "But I want your handling of Roy Hepburn done delicately. He is an old acquaintance."

My detectives were stunned at the revelation.

"Chief, we're sorry, but you can't say that; we have to be able to do our jobs without interference," Alissa and Ray both pushed.

I was silent; I felt crushed inside. I knew they were right, but then I tried to defend Roy in a subtle way.

"We have been assuming that the intruder is in his comfort zone and therefore living in the Southeast Section. What if we are wrong about that? Couldn't he live in the Northeast Section and do more of his dirty work in the Southeast Section to throw us off track?"

"Perhaps, Chief. Let's look at the list again. I have

updated it to cover all the crimes to date," Alissa offered.

"If that will help to make my point, yes, Alissa, let's look at it."

Glendale District
Lake Drive Circle

NW Section
47 Parks, K.D.
45 White, P.T.
43 West, H.D.
41 Evans, M.R.
39 Sharpe, A.L.
37 Monroe, G.K.
35 Schell, J.D.
33 McCray, K.L.
31 Clay, T.G.

NE Section
11 Green, K.D.
13 Hopper, M.A.
15 Grady, J.M.
17 Rivers, R.W.
19 Cannon, W.T.
21 Hicks, D.A.
23 Savage, L.T.**
25 Mobley, F.R.*
27 Newman, J.F.**
29 Kelly, E.S.

SW Section
11 Tracy, R.O.
13 Terry, G.D.
15 Walsh, T.M.
17 Parker, T.S.
19 Shay, T.J.*
21 Lester, E.P.
23 Vogel, H.K.
25 Usher, P.F.
27 Brown, D.H.
29 Dent, H.K.

SE Section
31 Hepburn, R.S.
33 Kimble, T.M.*
35 Stevens, A.B.**
37 Lenz, R.S.*
39 Burns, D.A.
41 Harley, M.D.*
43 Shaw, R.B.**
45 King, R.L.
47 Mosher, H.D.

"I've included Jane Newman, as you can see."

194

"Chief, this is a useless exercise," Ray said.

"Perhaps, Ray, but I feel we can't overlook anything," I pushed.

"Here are the last two cases in our brief report form," Alissa said.

Case number 8 – # 35 LDC Southeast Section (Serious)

Owner: Linda Savage, age, mid-twenties

Details: On November 10th, accosted in her home. Savagely beaten, raped and nearly strangled to death. We've gone over the details previously, so I won't repeat them, except to add that Linda is twenty-six, and works at the University.

Case number 9 – # 27 LDC Northeast Section (Serious)

Owner: Jane Newman

Details: November 18th. Murder victim number one for this intruder. Newman horribly beaten, raped and strangled. Further details are on file from the post-mortem.

"Chief, I don't see how this list supports your premise. Hepburn could easily work both sections. It isn't as though the sections are separated by fences. They blend from one to the other," Alissa pushed.

"But it could also be Harry West, have you forgotten that?"

"No, Chief, I haven't but I think we have more evidence, circumstantial or otherwise, against Hepburn than West at this point."

"Well, I'm not so sure. We…"

"Chief, you have to recuse yourself from this investigation."

"I know, Ray, you are right. I just can't accept that someone I've known for most of my life could be a cold-blooded killer. You will have to lead the investigation with no input from me. In fact, all information from this date forward should be held back from me. I won't be able to stand it, but it must be done. I will clear this with the DA, so I don't jeopardize the case."

"Let me speak with the District Attorney," Ray said, "I think your involvement is vital from an overall directional approach. Whenever it touches Roy, you will not have a controlling opinion. Fair enough?"

"Fair enough."

Later that day, Ray informed me that any investigative information would be provided to the DA before I would be allowed to see it. If DA Smith approved, then I would get a look at the evidence, but not a say in how it was to be handled. Also, the DA insisted that my conversations with his office would have to be at arms-length, so that anything I needed to discuss would be with Assistant DA Anthony Fuller.

Chapter Twenty-Four

Ray had convinced District Attorney Smith that enough circumstantial evidence related to Roy justified our requests for search warrants to be issued. The warrants were approved by Judge Arnold.

Within an hour, my friend, my mentor, Roy Hepburn was brought into the station for questioning while the searches were happening.

"Mister Hepburn we need to ask you some questions," Ray began.

"I need to ask you a question; what is this all about? The officers who came to me house wouldn't tell me any details; just you wanted to talk to me. I demand to speak to the Police Chief."

"That's not possible, Mister Hepburn. You need to speak with us."

"And if I won't?"

"We have gotten warrants to search your house and car. If you don't want to talk to us, the evidence will," Ray said.

"What evidence?"

"Your involvement with these burglaries and attacks."

"So I'm a suspect? I think I may need a lawyer."

"We are trying to eliminate suspects from our investigations," Ray answered.

"I am not involved with any of them."

"If you're willing to talk to us, Mister Hepburn, Detective Riley will read you your Miranda Rights."

"Is that necessary?"

"It is; Roy, our procedures require us to routinely do that. It prevents any misunderstanding on our part in the future. We want to be able to eliminate you as a suspect."

"Okay, shoot."

Alissa then read him his rights. Roy agreed to speak with my detectives until he felt the need for a lawyer.

"Roy, do you know a Frances Mobley?"

"I'm quite sure I do; I think she lives in the Northeast section. Doesn't she?"

"How do you know her?"

"Well, I've been to her house a couple of times."

"You have? Why?"

"She invited me."

"Why would a twenty-something woman invite a man of your age to her home?"

"I guess she liked me; is that a crime?"

"No, but it seems strange for a young woman to ask you. What did you do when you visited?"

"We talked and drank some wine. I usually brought a bottle, but she always had some on hand. After we were done, I went home."

"Roy, what does 'after we were done,' mean?"

"Well, you know what wine can do to people."

"No, tell us what it means."

"It means we may have lost our heads some evenings."

"How many times did this happen?"

"A few; I don't keep count."

"When was the last time you 'visited' her?"

"Maybe a month back. I can't really remember."

"You can't remember the last time you went to bed with a pretty young woman?" Alissa asked disbelievingly.

"Do you remember every guy you've been with?"

"We ask the questions, Roy, not you," Ray interjected.

"So, Roy, when was it?" Alissa asked again.

"Well, it may have been around the time Franny had an unexpected night visitor. I'm not saying it was for sure, but…"

"So it wasn't you who crept into her cottage?"

"Of course not, I was always invited."

"How do you know about the visitor?"

"How do you think? She called me the next day."

"Why would she call you, Roy?"

"Because, I am someone that she trusts."

"Do others in Glendale trust you, Roy?"

"Yes, men and women both."

"Who are some of the others?"

"I'm not saying. That would violate a trust."

"Okay, Roy, let's try this; does Maureen Shay trust you?"

"Well, yes."

"Does her husband?"

"He doesn't really know me."

"So how come Maureen knows you, but her husband doesn't?"

"He's not there when we visit."

"He's not there?"

"No, he works and she calls me over."

"So what do you and Maureen do?"

"What do you think we do? Do I have to spell it out?"

"No, please don't, Roy; we get the picture," Alissa said.

"Let's try another," Ray suggested, "Do you know Rebecca Shaw?"

"I do; she's been a friend since I moved in."

"Roy, she is a college student. How old was she when she became your friend?"

"She's a friend? How friendly?"

"She was a teenager; her father, Bob, is really my friend, not her. His job required him to move to another city, but he lets her live there while she's going to the University. He asked me to watch out for her."

"Was it you in her cottage that night? Were you there to have sex with her and she didn't want it?"

"Are you crazy? I get enough without hitting on college students."

"Since you seem to get around in Glendale, perhaps you thought it was something a young woman would be…"

"You have got to be kidding with that question. Are you so hung up on things I do in my private life?"

"No, Roy, but since she is a friend, we want to know when you last saw her."

"She called me the next day after somebody came to her cottage in the middle of the night. She gave me all the details."

"So, you know that he tried to strangle her."

"She didn't tell me that."

"What did she tell you?"

"She told me that a guy broke in through her back door and came into her bedroom. She screamed and he ran away. She couldn't tell much about him."

"Have you been to the cottage since Bob moved out?"

"I know what you are implying, but no. That would be wrong. You don't seem to understand that I have standards."

"Well, there is married Maureen, Roy. What standards are you employing there?"

"Forget it. You don't understand."

"No, we probably don't; have you talked to Rebecca since that day?"

"I call her every day to be sure she is okay. I also speak to Bob who is very concerned. He says to stay close to her. I promised I will. She has one year left before she graduates. He wants me to help her find a roommate. She has a boyfriend, but Bob doesn't want him to live with her, so we are looking for a dependable female."

"Okay, Roy, have you ever been in cottage number 23 in the Northeast section?"

"I may have, but I'm not sure. Why?"

"Do you know a Linda Savage?"

"Who? No, I don't think so."

"So, you've never had wine and whatever with her?"

"I just said I don't know her."

"She seems to know you."

"When I say 'know' I mean that I sometimes socialize with the person. I don't 'know' Linda."

"Well, then how does she 'know' you?"

"I did a job for her awhile back. I replaced locks on her doors. It was after your flyer went out. She got nervous and decided that she needed changes to her locks."

"What kind of locks did you install?"

"I put in strong locks. They're very difficult to pick, not impossible for someone who knows them, but tricky."

"But you could pick them?"

"Of course, but I have no need for that. I give the owner a set of keys stamped 'do not dup' and keep a copy in case they should lose their keys."

"That's quite convenient, Roy. It means you have access to those homes."

"If you think about it, Detective, I have access to any house I want, but that doesn't mean I do."

"Have you ever been in Linda's cottage since you replaced the locks?"

"No!"

"Let's move on. Have you ever been to Abigail Stevens' house?"

"Which house is hers?"

"Hey, Smart Guy, it's two doors down from your cottage. You know damn well where she lives. Now answer my question: have you ever been to Abigail Stevens' home?"

"Yes, Detective, I have. She and her boyfriend invited

several neighbors over for drinks one evening. This was before somebody hurt her."

"Is that the only time?"

"I believe so."

"You believe so. What room in her cottage did you all meet for drinks?"

"I think it was the living room."

"Did you go out to the patio?"

"Not that I can recall."

"We have several fingerprints of yours on the door jamb of the back door. Care to explain how they came to be there?"

"Oh, that's right; I replaced her locks a month or so ago."

"The woman who discovered Miss Stevens that morning went to Mister Burn's cottage for help. Why didn't she come to you?"

"I don't know who you are talking about. I had a falling out with Stevens sometime ago. She thought I was trying to be fresh with her. I wasn't, but I couldn't convince her."

"A falling out. So, you tried to put the make on her also."

"I did not; I don't care what she says."

"What the woman did say to us is that you seemed to know a lot about the injuries to Miss Stevens. Why do you suppose she would think that?"

"You're lying to me. I don't even know who you are talking about."

"What do you think happened to Miss Stevens?"

"I don't really know, but I assumed that Miss Stevens had been raped."

"Why would you assume that, Roy?"

"From the grapevine in the neighborhood, the guy is getting more and more violent."

"Roy, do you know Jane Newman?"

"Yes, and before you ask, I have been to her house. I did some work at her house several weeks ago."

"What kind of work, Roy?"

"I changed her front and back door locks. She has been very nervous about what's been going on in the area."

"So you have keys to her home also?"

"It's what I do."

"When was the last time you saw her?"

"It was a few days before someone murdered her. I couldn't believe it."

"Roy, this isn't looking good for you."

"Look; people in Glendale have called me to do many odd jobs for them including locks. That's why it's hard to remember every home I've been to. Your questions are confusing me. Harry West and I take care of the neighborhood."

"I bet you do. We need to take a break, Roy. Can I get you a sandwich or something?"

Chapter Twenty-Five

"Alissa, I think Hepburn is our man. When we go back in, I want to cover the Jane Newman killing in depth with him. We didn't release many details of her murder. If he slips, we've got him."

"I agree, Ray, and we have some details coming in about the search of his house, which, by the way, is a mess according to the forensics team."

"What have they found so far?"

"For one, there is quite a collection of women's underwear; all neatly folded and put in dresser drawers and boxes."

"All kinds of underwear?"

"All kinds and they are different sizes."

"Anything else?"

"Yes, buried underneath the underwear in one drawer were several photographs of a man and woman, both naked. The man is raping the woman whose hands are tied behind her back. Forensics says you can't see the man or woman's faces."

"That bastard, I can see the noose getting closer to his neck. I can't wait."

"Ray, I am beginning to feel sorry for the Chief. His friend, a killer and a pervert."

"I am also, but…"

"Ray, I talked to the Chief about Roy; nothing specific, but I feel that we should let him talk with Roy. It may help us to get a confession. Chief has asked the DA and he said a short visit with one of us present is okay if nothing specific is discussed about the cases."

"I'm surprised that the DA agreed."

"Let's get back to Hepburn. Did he want anything for lunch?" Alissa said.

"No, I think the pressure is beginning to wear him down. I hope we can get a confession out of him, but he thinks he is smarter than we are. Let's go."

"So, Roy, are you sure we can't get you something to eat or drink?"

"No, I don't want anything. How much longer is this charade going to take? I am getting tired."

"Not too much longer if you are honest with us."

"I have been very honest with you two. I don't like that insinuation at all."

"Well, we're sorry you feel that way, but we keep finding out things that make us wonder."

"Such as?"

"As you know, we are conducting a search of your car and house. What we have…"

"I think I need a lawyer."

"That's your right. If you want, you can call one. What do you want to do?"

"What if I call a lawyer, what happens next?"

"We will get an arrest warrant and you will be charged with committing multiple B&E's, rape, and torture of several women and the murder of Jane Newman."

"I didn't murder Jane Newman. I didn't do any break-ins. I'm not a rapist or murderer."

"Do you still want a lawyer?"

"I'll wait."

"From our search of your cottage, Roy, we know that you like porn. Worse, you like to take movies of yourself while raping a woman."

"That's a lie, you bastard."

"It's not a lie, Roy, we found many tapes of you and others. Also, you have quite a collection of women's undergarments like bras and panties. Sound familiar?"

"Those are my wife's clothes. I didn't have the heart to throw them out after she was murdered."

"So, how many different sizes of underclothing did your wife wear?" Alissa asked with a smirk.

"You didn't have anything to do with your wife's murder, did you?" Ray pushed.

"You are a son-of-a-bitch, of course not."

"I think you are lying to us about a lot of things, Roy."

"I'm not lying to you."

"We find your fingerprint evidence at houses where burglaries have occurred. That makes us suspicious; you are a locksmith, which makes us even more suspicious."

"Yes, but that doesn't prove anything."

"It doesn't prove when you were at those places, but it proves that you were there, which may be enough."

"Why are you trying to pin these things on me?"

"We aren't, Roy, we let the facts do that."

"You don't have much."

"We would like to ask you when you were at Jane Newman's cottage last?"

"I was there a few days before she was murdered. You must have found my prints. I changed her door locks."

"How convenient, Roy, how convenient."

"You know what? You should dust for prints on many other cottage doors because I have replaced many."

"We just may do that, Roy."

"You'll find I've been a help to people especially after you put the fear of God in them with your flyer."

"Do you still want a lawyer?"

"Not right now."

"Are you still willing to talk to us?"

"I will, if I can talk to Chief Connor."

"Okay, Roy, if he is willing; I will get him. I'll be right back."

After Alissa called me, I went to the interview room. Alissa remained with me.

"I want to talk to you alone."

"No, Roy, she stays."

"Robbie, why are you doing this to me?"

"Roy, we can't talk about anything specific concerning the cases. What I can recommend to you is that you tell my detectives everything you know. They will do the right thing, but you must be honest with them."

"I never thought that you would let me down like this, Robbie. All that I have done for you over the years means nothing to you? We are friends, don't you remember?"

"You are wrong, Roy, dead wrong. Anne and I will always consider you the close friend that you are. I just can't intercede for you now. It would be very wrong."

"I can't believe you would betray me this way. You are a traitor to your friends. After all I did for you."

"What do you expect me to do, Roy? You have left…"

"Chief, I think we can't continue this any longer."

"Okay, Detective. Roy, I wish you the best. Goodbye."

"Yeah, Robbie, you wish me the best. You could get these goons…"

"That's not what I can do. Goodbye, Roy," I interrupted, while walking out.

Ray entered the room.

"Then I want a lawyer now; I'm done talking."

"Roy, are you sure?" Ray asked.

"You're damn right I am."

"Roy Hepburn, I am detaining you pending an arrest warrant being issued for the murder of Jane Newman. That and other charges will be filed with the District Attorney."

"Do you have an attorney or will you need…?" Alissa started to ask.

"I want Sam Goldman; I don't want some young snot out of law school."

"Here's the phone; call him."

I was to get my first viewing of the evidence against Roy and needed to discuss it with the Assistant District Attorney, Anthony Fuller.

"Anthony, I want to talk to you about the latest suspect

we have for the burglaries and attacks on the women in the District."

"Michael told me that you and this Hepburn are friends, is that true?"

"Unfortunately, Anthony, it's true. It is hard for me to admit, but it's true."

"I can appreciate what you must be going through, but from the evidence I have seen to date, Rob, you have a strong circumstantial case against Hepburn, but not enough for us to try to prosecute. You have no proof that the clothing found in his cottage belongs to any of the women attacked. No proof at all. I can't work miracles. You need solid proof that the tapes and the clothing found are what you are alleging, especially since your interviews with the local women are backing up his version of events. I'm sorry, Rob, keep working."

"But Anthony, we know it's him."

"You don't, Chief, you just think you do. Keep working. I'll say something that you already know, Rob. The circumstantial evidence that your detectives have found against Harry West is just as strong."

"Yes, I know. Having two strong suspects is worse than having no suspects."

"In this case, then you can't arrest two men for suspicious activities related to the same crimes."

"I know, Anthony, I know. It's just…"

"There is no way that we can support any arrest warrants at this time. You somehow have to enough probable cause to separate your suspicions of West from Hepburn. It's a hell of a bad situation for you, but…"

"Unless we can get a confession from one of them, a killer is going to walk."

"Well, you can't water-board them, so what's left?"

"Honestly, Anthony, at this point, I just do not know."

I left the DA's Office knowing that more women would be put at risk because we could not get the system to act.

So, unfortunately for us, no judge would issue a warrant. No evidence other than Roy's and West's fingerprints was found at the cottages and that could be explained in view of their odd-job businesses.

Roy did keep reasonable books. His entries for lock replacements at sundry cottages validated his answers he gave at the interrogation. My intuition and bias could play no role here.

Worse for Ray and Alissa's hard work at interviewing, none of the victims could identify Roy or West as the burglar. The women they had been "familiar" with all corroborated their stories.

Roy's brief detention was over and he was immediately released. I hoped the violence would stop or at least take a long break. I left the station that day very depressed.

Later that evening, Anne and I talked about what had happened.

"I'm sure that Roy will never forgive me for what took place today, Anne."

"From what you said, I can understand it."

"You don't appreciate the problem, Anne; my hands were tied by the DA. I couldn't be a part of any of that process without destroying any reasonable chance of convicting Roy, if he was guilty. My career would be toast, and you know it."

"I know, Rob, but couldn't it have been handled better?"

"Anne, I don't want to argue about this. Roy has dirty hands. Maybe they're not murderous hands, but they are dirty, nevertheless."

"What do you mean dirty?"

"He seems to be screwing a lot of the women in Glendale; he says they are willing. The problem I have with his behavior is his preoccupation with sex."

"Rob, don't be a prude; he's single, probably lonely and you know what. Besides, you're not exactly…"

"No, but we're married, Anne."

"Have you interviewed the women that he says he…?"

"Yes, we've talked to them, and to the woman they defend Roy."

"So, what's the crime?"

"We did a search of his cottage. He has drawers and boxes full of women's underwear. Different sizes, for God's sake! What does that say to you?"

"Did his women conquests say he stole their panties or did they give them to him?"

"They did. Why? I can't understand. What about your thought that someone had stolen some of your things from our house?"

"I don't know, Rob, maybe I was wrong about that. But Roy did tell me one time that he never threw out Heidi's personals; he just didn't want to part with them. She had money and apparently she bought loads of them. He also bought sexy things for her."

"Okay, so he is a Don Juan. He may also be a killer."

"Rob, for God's sake, you don't believe that?"

"I don't want to, but there are just too many unanswered questions about him."

"Rob, you've been in law enforcement for a long time now. If he is guilty, he will make a mistake; if he isn't, let's hope the guilty one will. Rest on that. See what you can do to mend our friendship with him."

"I will try, Anne, but I don't know if I can continue with this job."

"I understand, Rob, do what you have to do."

Chapter Twenty-Six

I knew that Anne was right. I had to find a way to reestablish my friendship with Roy. If Roy could understand that I could not direct the investigation because we were friends, it might be possible. Asking Roy to forgive and forget was almost certainly futile, but I had to try. Worse, I was only trying to patch up our relationship to catch him in a mistake. This deceitful tactic was probably the only way to get Roy to slip up, but I was betraying the trust and friendship of one who had done so much for me. The guilt of that haunted me to the end.

My shame also stemmed from my treatment of my detectives. I had knowingly tried to thwart the direction of their work to save a friend. It was not professional behavior and it was a crime, which I would have to face one day.

However, whether Roy was a friend or not, I was still a police officer. Roy was a solid suspect in terrible crimes. I had to stop him.

First, I had to restore the trust of my detectives. So, the next morning, I called Ray and Alissa for a meeting to assuage my conscience and to discuss my plan for handling Roy.

"Chief, before you say anything, Ray and I want you to know that we understand what you are going through."

"Alissa is right. When we became aware that you have a longtime relationship with Roy Hepburn, we knew…"

"I can't say how much this means to me. I had planned to come her today to say that I felt I had to resign. I tried to

214

mislead…"

Alissa interrupted, "Look, Chief, what you did, was not a big deal, especially since Ray and I realized your reluctance to accept our theory about where the murderer lives. We did a little investigating on our own, so we knew about you and Hepburn. We simply worked around that."

"In fact, Chief, you did us a favor because you inadvertently pointed us in the right direction by your…"

"Ray is saying that we need to put this problem behind us and move on," Alissa interrupted again.

"I don't know what to say. You are the best people I have ever worked with."

"Okay, Chief, what do we do from here?"

"I guess that I don't need to tell you we are facing a real crisis. With no solid proof against either Hepburn or West, I am thinking that we may have to use a less accepted strategy."

"Chief, if Judge Arnold had given us the warrant, we could have had time to develop a case," Ray interrupted with genuine disgust.

"I second that feeling; he has put the community at great risk," Alissa ventured.

"I couldn't agree more, Folks, but the real question is what we do next. I have a suggestion; I want to…"

"I want to spend time on the photographs found in Hepburn's cottage. He is a clever one, that Hepburn; cropped off his head in the photos so he couldn't be identified; positioned the women so that their faces were away from the camera," Ray again interrupted me.

"If we could have booked him, we could have gotten photos of his body. Plus, the tapes we found may have helped," I added.

"The forensics people are trying to find something unique about him to compare with the photos we think he took of Savage and Stevens; no luck yet," Alissa offered.

"Alissa, I'm bothered about the assumption that the women in the photos are Savage and Stevens. What does forensics say about that?"

"As Ray said, unfortunately, the women's faces were positioned away from the camera enough to prevent a positive identification of the women."

"These pictures aren't of any evidence value if they can't be used to positively ID the women."

"You're right, Chief, I think that's a dead-end unless…"

"Okay, okay, hold off for a moment. If Hepburn is the killer, I have a plan. I want to reestablish my friendship with Hepburn, if possible."

"Chief, what are you thinking? That will jeopardize our case if we do find some conclusive evidence," Ray pushed.

"Well, what we are doing now hasn't worked, has it?"

"No, but…"

"Look, if I can regain his confidence, maybe he will slip up somehow; I don't know, but isn't it worth a try?"

"I don't feel comfortable with this idea, Chief," Alissa rejoined.

"I feel that my association with Hepburn has shackled

us. If that is the case, then let's use it to our advantage. I can carry a wire at some point.

"There are a number of facts about Newman's murder that we haven't made public. We did the same with the Savage and Steven's break-ins. He is bound to slip up if I can gain his confidence again."

"Do you really think that is going to happen? He's going to welcome you back with open arms? With all due respect, Chief, you need to get real," Alissa said with emphasis I had not expected from her.

"Perhaps not, do you have a better idea?"

"The thing I suggest is that we grind through these cases as we do in every other; hard work, follow-up on any lead, and don't make mistakes," Ray said.

"Well, I suggest the following: use my plan, use your plan, and keep surveillance of both West and Hepburn operational. As you know, Jason Green isn't out of the picture, either," I stressed.

"No, they aren't, but we weren't able to obtain any naked photos of Green, West, or Hepburn so forensics can't evaluate them."

"That's not exactly true, Alissa. Remember that we found porn on West's computer. He likes to have himself photographed," Ray interjected.

"Did we save any of that?"

"No, Chief, DA Smith said to delete any copies we had, so they're gone."

"Too bad, Alissa, and we can't establish a personal

relationship with West."

"So, perhaps we can get one of West's friends to carry a wire," Ray tried to make clear with some satisfaction.

"Better yet, Chief, what if we can get one of his paramours to participate in his photo shoots?" Alissa added.

"Do you have any names?" I probed.

"West mentioned a Margaret Bowen; she lives on Parker Street here in the City."

"Have we talked to her?"

"Yes, she was West's alibi for the night Newman was killed."

"Do you believe her?"

"She answered my questions with some hesitation, so I'm not sure she's being honest."

"Do you believe she would work with us?"

"Chief, I believe that I can talk her into it. I sensed that she was uncomfortable about being his alibi for the night Newman was killed. She did tell me that West is sometimes rough with her. I think there is no love lost there."

"So, why does she go to bed with him?"

"Who knows? Momentary thrills? No morals? I don't know."

"We have to be careful there; entrapment would be a lawyer's rant," I cautioned.

"You need to test the idea with Smith; you also need to ask him about your plan with Hepburn, Chief," Ray advised.

"I'll get to the DA after we break. In the meantime, Alissa, test the waters with this Bowen. Make it sound as if it's her idea. It would be embarrassing if she were to double cross us."

"Okay, Chief, I'll go to see her."

"Before we break, I am concerned that we may be too close to certain ideas. I fear that we are not open-minded enough."

"What are you getting at, Chief?" Ray asked.

"I have pushed the idea that it has to be the same person committing the burglaries, the murder of Newman, the rape of Stevens, and the Savage crime. What if that is not true?"

"Honestly, Chief, unless we can get some hard evidence on someone in either scenario, it is hopeless to speculate."

"I agree, Ray, but I want us to work from the standpoint now that we may be dealing with two intruders. He may be one who just likes thrills and the other out to rape and murder. Just keep it in mind."

"Chief, you wouldn't be thinking about your friend, Roy, would you? Perhaps, you're hoping that he is only the burglar and not a killer?"

"No, Alissa, it's just that I may have pushed us into limiting our vision, so that it is impairing how we investigate these cases."

"Well, I believe that we are doing all that we can, regardless of whether it's one or two culprits."

"I know, Ray, I'm not saying that we aren't doing good investigative work, it's just…"

"Chief, again with all due respect, please back away from this investigation a bit, let us do our work. I personally believe that Roy Hepburn is the killer and rapist," Alissa said with conviction.

"Okay, okay, Alissa. My promise to you and Ray is this: I will do my best to prove or disprove Roy's guilt; I will support your position whatever direction our investigation takes us. Let's follow up on the West plan. You work to prove that West is guilty. I will push my plan with Hepburn. Perhaps something will come of them."

"I hope you'll pardon this comment, Chief, but this whole situation is beginning to feel like the Stooges. The only things we're missing are the pies to smash into each other's faces," Ray said with a sneer.

"I know, Ray, I've been thinking the same thing. We have no hard evidence for any of the cases, yet we spin from person to person, calling them suspects with our unsupported accusations. I'm not feeling very professional right now."

"Well, if we can achieve any concrete results with our present direction, then our plans are not so silly, but…"

"What do we do about Green?" Alissa asked.

"I think we have enough on our plates right now."

Chapter Twenty-Seven

After our meeting ended, I arranged an appointment with DA Smith for the afternoon. The consultation went as well as I could have expected.

Michael Smith's admonitions were these: don't break any laws; don't endanger the investigations of suspects by entrapping them; don't mistakenly divulge any crime information that is not already in the public domain; and finally, don't offer any special treatment for cooperation by witnesses or suspects.

Armed with all those "don'ts," I proceeded to let Alissa and Ray know of the meeting results. We had a tentative "go ahead" with the understanding that I never heard it from the DA.

As part of my plan, I called Abner.

"Abner, Robbie here. I wanted to let you know that we had to let our two prime suspects walk, at least for now. I was wondering if your informant has had a change of heart about Hepburn's involvement in the burglaries out here."

"Coincidentally Robbie, I just had a conversation with my source about him and the answer is no. Hepburn is the guilty one."

"Is he guilty of the murder or just the burglaries?"

"My informant says both."

"That is depressing, Abner. I had hoped your informant had made a mistake."

"Nope, sorry."

"Well, thank you, Abner."

"A piece of advice, Robbie, don't let him get away."

"We'll do our best."

After the call ended, I agonized about Abner's mysterious source. Who could it be? How did he know that much about our cases? It did not make sense that an outsider could know that much.

"Still," I thought, "they have resources and informants we can only dream about."

Later that evening at home, I made the difficult call to Roy. When he heard my voice, he hung up. This was going to be much more difficult than I thought. If I couldn't even get him to say hello, how would I ever get him to open up?

Anne had the suggestion that she would try to mend the relationship by visiting him. I knew that Roy admired Anne. I thought it might work, but with his anger at me, I was very worried that he might harm her.

"No, Anne, I don't think that is a good idea. What if he takes his anger out on you?"

"I'll be armed, you know that, Rob."

"I know that, but he also knows that. What if he drugs your drink or something?"

"You're imagining things, Rob. He won't hurt me."

"Look, Anne, Abner has an informant who says that Roy is the killer. I can't let you do that."

"Let me try. You have my back."

"Calling him is one thing, Anne, but going over to his house alone is another."

"No, Rob, I am going to do it. You are not stopping me.

Your whole personality has changed during this investigation. We have to fix it."

"I can't stop you from this foolishness?"

"No, you can't. That's final. I am going to call him right now and go over there."

With that, she called Roy. He listened and invited her to come to his cottage.

"Anne, I want to go with you. I can stay in the car, if he does something, I can stop him."

"No, you stay here. If I need you, which I won't, I'll call."

"Anne, you are wrong, wrong! Don't do it, please. This guy has brutally killed a young woman. What makes you think he won't...?"

"It's eight-thirty now. I'll be back by ten."

With that, she left. I felt useless as a husband. I couldn't even talk my wife out of doing something dangerous, and yes, silly. Still, she had been right about many things in our marriage.

Why did I doubt her now? Of course, before I had never felt her decisions could be life-threatening.

The time went excruciatingly slow, and before I knew it, ten o'clock had arrived. By ten-thirty, I was frantic. Time to take the cruiser and go to Roy's house.

When I reached his house, Anne was just walking to her car. Roy was walking beside her. When he saw the cruiser, he stopped and waved. I could not believe it.

I stepped out of the car. Roy approached me with an

outreached hand, which I shook with great relief.

"Roy, I am so sorry about all of this."

"Anne, clarified things, Robbie, let it go. I understand."

We made plans to see Roy on Saturday afternoon. He would come to our house for dinner. I felt so relieved that Roy had come to his senses.

Later, I asked Anne what had happened.

"Let's just say that I was able to satisfy him, Rob. By the way, his house is definitely a bachelor pad."

"And that means?"

"Nothing, Rob, it's just an observation."

"Care to tell me more about satisfying him?" I asked with a tinge of jealousy.

"Rob, get serious. We just talked. Sometimes I think you are losing it over this case. Goodnight."

The next morning, I met with Alisa and Ray to share the news. My conscience wouldn't let me forget that the meetings with Roy from this point on were deceptive and meant to bring my one-time friend to justice. It was a form of torture I had willingly agreed to, but I wasn't sure I wanted to live through it.

"If he is coming over on Saturday, what is your plan?" Alissa started.

"Nothing specific, some reminiscence chatter, I hope. I have to get his confidence back. It's going to take some time. I have to tell you both that this whole plan is putting a huge stress on me. He called me a traitor and the words won't go away. He's right, I am."

"Chief, first and foremost, you are a professional. It is tragic that your friend is a rapist and murderer. It is your duty to stop him by any means. This plan is just one of those means," Alissa said, trying to encourage and comfort me.

"I appreciate your kind words, Alissa. I need all the strength I can garner."

"You know that Agent Smith says that Roy is still the number one suspect," Ray added, "We can't forget that."

"Yes, Ray, that is one of the reasons I can even think about doing this."

"I know this can't happen on Saturday, but let's talk about what your approach with him should be over time," Alissa ventured.

"As I said earlier, Saturday is small talk. If he brings up the past few days with us, which he will, I will deflect it to avoid any details, especially in front of Anne."

"That's wise, Chief."

"At some point, I suggest the next time I meet with him; I will drop a false hint that Newman's hands had been bound but we aren't sure what was used. We know they were tie-wrapped, but we didn't let that info out. I want to do anything we can to nail him. He must be stopped, friend or no friend."

"You will be wearing a wire when that happens, right?"

"Not directly, I've already had the tech guys over to place bugs in several rooms for that purpose. You'll be able to monitor and record what's said. We will have to set up a schedule for the detective group, including you two."

"What if he wants to talk about the cases on Saturday?"

"As I said, I will try to deflect it; I don't want him to start suspecting anything, or probing me for information."

"Okay, Chief, I volunteer to monitor Saturday," Ray offered, "Marie is visiting our daughter this weekend."

"Alissa, how is your plan coming along?"

"Well, I talked to Bowen as we discussed. She is uncomfortable about having us see any photos he might take of them doing it, so to speak, but she says she will if it catches a killer."

"What people won't do for fifteen minutes of fame," Ray said.

"Have you set it up yet?"

"No, we talked about when; she thinks it won't be until next week."

"I can see this not working out, Chief."

"Well, Ray, what do you suggest?"

"I have no better idea, I guess."

"Well, once the Bowen thing is set up, Alissa, get us the details. We only need a photo of West for comparison to the other prints we have… Oh, that's right we had to destroy our copies, right?"

"Right, Chief."

"So, what we want Bowen to do is to try to get him to tell her about what he likes to do with women?"

"Photos and that, yes," Alissa answered.

Chapter Twenty-Eight

Saturday evening came and went without any difficulties arising during our dinner with Roy. Nevertheless, I would have to say the conversations were stilted, and that is an understatement. Each of us used guarded language and refrained from any talk tangentially touching the Newman murder, or the Savage and Stevens cases.

Roy had lost his glibness. His automatic comeback comments to my friendly jibes were lost that evening. After Roy had left, Anne and I tried to assess what had occurred.

"Rob, I can see that things will never be back to what they were. You are both bleeding inside."

"Yes, he was cold. My silly jokes didn't raise a smile out of him. You're right, of course, it was naïve of me to think that I could push the water back. Notice that he only had one beer this evening. That's very unusual for him."

"Well, Rob, he obviously didn't want to loosen up enough to fall into your sophomoric trap."

"It hurts a bit to hear you say that, but in retrospect, it was a silly idea of mine. Ray and Alissa warned me about it. I thought that reconnecting was possible, since Roy and I went back so far."

"No, I thought we could repair the outer damage, Rob, but I never felt that trust would ever be fully restored between you two. It is obvious that you don't trust him. Don't you think he feels the same way?"

"I know that. I wish it weren't so. I don't know where

we go from here."

"My suggestion, Rob, is that we continue to be as friendly as we can with Roy. You will have to give up the idea that you can trap him into saying something incriminating. It is not going to work that way."

"Yeah, I agree. The Newman murder case is going to become red-hot very soon. Her parents are bigwigs who are connected to the Governor. It'll flow downhill pretty fast."

"What's your plan?"

"Damn it all, Anne, I don't have a plan. This was it! This miserable failure you witnessed tonight. As much as I want it, he's not going to trust me anymore."

"Say goodnight, Rob, it will look better in the morning."

With that, I spent a restless night. On Monday morning, I met with Ray and Alissa.

"Well, Ray, you heard it all Saturday night. We've got nothing from Roy."

"You expected too much from the first get-together. I warned you. My advice is to listen to Anne and continue your socials with Roy. If he is going to slip, it will take time."

"So, what you are really saying, Ray, is that we wait for him to kill again."

"There is no other way, Chief. We have done all that we can to warn people. If they can't understand that they must protect themselves, I can only feel disgust, but that is their decision."

"That's callous, Ray," Alissa interjected.

"Well then, Alissa, tell us how your little plan is working out," Ray retorted.

"Come on, Folks, it does no good for us to be at each other's throats," I admonished, but I felt the same frustrations they had.

"My update of the plan having Bowen compromise West is going nowhere. After I had talked to her, she and West got into an argument over something; she doesn't want any part of our harebrained scheme, as she put it."

"I understand, Alissa. I guess Ray is right. We must wait for the next murder and hope the killer makes a big mistake. I want the patrols increased in the District."

"We are nearly maxed out now, Chief."

"Ray, I don't care. I can't have another woman's murder on my conscience. We have got to prevent…"

"I'll do my best, Chief. Be prepared to approve a lot of overtime."

"If that is what it takes, then do it. How I handle the political pressure will be challenging."

"Chief, I am really curious about the FBI's informant. How does this person know as much as they seem to know without being involved?"

"I've assumed that the FBI has resources and reaches deeper than we can into this sordid world."

"Chief, Agent Smith says the person is reliable in their accusation of Roy, but how does that person know for sure?"

"The only explanation I have is that the informant must

live in Glendale."

"Are you saying the informant is close enough to have witnessed the killing?"

"Maybe, Alissa, but I believe that this informant has witnessed something, which they are afraid to bring to us out of fear for their own life."

"But then, why go to the FBI? They have no jurisdiction here and they can't protect a witness."

"Oh, but they can, Alissa. They are very good with their Witness Protection program. The FBI is very good at keeping their informants or witnesses, as you may prefer, out of the light and danger," I reminded them.

"I think it's criminal, Chief, not to give us the identity of this informant."

"From our point of view, Ray, I agree with you, but Agent Smith said the FBI's concerns are more important. I have no way to judge that. They are working a huge case affecting not only national, but possibly international crimes. There is no way we could ever stop that train, even if we wanted to. But it appalls me how some little jerk in Augusta can be so involved in our murder investigation is a mystery to me. Agent Smith apparently can say no more."

"So, Chief, what now?"

"For one, I will keep working the Hepburn plan, such as it is. I'm not sure anything will work there, but it's all we have. I want to keep the surveillance of West and Hepburn going. The killer may lie low for a while, but he will strike again. He's not done, by a long shot."

"So, we wait for another woman to be raped and murdered," Alissa nearly shouted.

"Our hands are tied. Unless you have a better idea, yes."

"Chief, I know we are tending to zero in on Hepburn as the more probable guy, but something is bothering me."

"What's that, Ray?"

"We all know that the Northwest section of Glendale has not had any reported break-ins. West lives in that section. I believe that West is most likely the murderer. To throw us off track, he only hits the other sections. He doesn't want to dirty his own nest."

"Well, I've had another thought, which I haven't shared with you. I've had the feeling that West may be Agent Smith's informant."

"That's interesting, Alissa. We certainly have no proof and Agent Smith is not going to affirm it, if he is, but it makes some crazy sense."

"Well, Chief, it's the first crazy idea I like. Why do you believe that, Alissa?" Ray asked.

"What if West is the rapist and killer? Suppose he has contacted Agent Smith to accuse Hepburn of the crimes? That way he becomes protected by the FBI while still committing his crimes."

"Interesting idea, Alissa, but what would he have to do with the big FBI investigation?"

"Remember that West served time in jail for harming a woman. Suppose that, while in prison, he became involved with some inmate who gave him information that he knows

231

that the FBI needs."

"Hmm, your idea is not as far-fetched as I initially felt, Alissa. West feeds Agent Smith the information that he wants while pushing clues, which he alone knows, to incriminate Hepburn. That is a beautifully sinister plan."

"Wow! This idea fits perfectly."

"Yes, Ray, and as far as our crimes are concerned, West fits the profile very well. For one, we do know that West is into sadomasochistic activities with women that he knows. So, why wouldn't he like to actually have a woman he doesn't know under his power?"

"But, Chief, why did he need to kill Newman? Savage and Stevens said that they couldn't identify him because he blindfolds them. He does what he wants with them; they even cooperate for fear he will kill them. There's no need to kill," Ray asserted.

"If Newman saw his face, he would have to kill her. He raped and tortured her over several hours. Maybe he let her see his face. If so, I think she knew she was going to die. But, I think his need goes deeper than that. I believe that he wanted to see what it felt like to actually kill someone," I answered.

"That's so horrible to think about."

"It is, Alissa. We have nothing but our speculations about West. We are going to have to wait for his next move; I am sorry to say."

"Sometimes this job sucks."

"I agree, Ray, but there is nothing else we can do."

Chapter Twenty-Nine

The wait was agonizing. We believed that nothing might happen for some time and it hadn't. We had no sense how long the killer would wait until things settled down. It had been four months since Jane Newman had been murdered. Maybe the killer had moved on or abandoned his activities.

In frustration, I proposed another plan to the group. It was a bizarre plan, but the only one I could come up with. We needed to entice the killer, whoever it was, to strike. The only way was to lure him was with human bait, female bait.

"Chief, what you are proposing is very dangerous," Ray voiced. "And, by the way, illegal."

"Secondly, who the hell are you going to get to be this 'bait?' " Alissa asked indignantly.

"I know, Alissa, and it can't be you because both West and Hepburn know who you are. That's same reason that leaves Green, our other possible suspect, out also."

"Then who are you going to get?"

"I don't know yet. I wanted to ask if you could get behind this idea."

"I see nothing but the terrible downside, if things go wrong," Ray answered.

"I understand, Ray, but if it works, we have stopped a killer," Alissa expressed.

"Folks, I don't like this plan either, but we really have no choice. I don't want to wait any longer for him to pick some innocent person out. We must act."

"I don't know, Chief, I…"

"I fully understand, Ray, I will undertake this alone. You and Alissa will not be involved in the planning or execution of it. I ask that you not speak about it. If it fails, I will take the entire responsibility."

"It could mean arrest and trial for you."

"It could, but that does not…"

"I will be part of it," Alissa volunteered.

"No, I'd rather you weren't. I will do this alone."

What I did not tell them that day, was that I had already put a tentative strategy into play. I had met James Mills soon after I had taken the role as police chief in Alton. We both belonged to a local shooting club.

James and I became friends with common interests in guns and match shooting. Even considering the trip from Alton to Augusta, James and his fiancée, Mary Adams, were often guests at our house and we were at theirs. After all these years, I considered James and Mary to be friends in the sense that Roy had inspired in me. In fact, though, James had become a close friend. We shared interests and personal ambitions, which we never shared with Mary and Anne.

Both James and Mary were in their mid-thirties. They lived together and just hadn't gotten around to tying the knot. Mary was very attractive with a slender body, blond hair and blue eyes, which made her the type of woman the killer seemed to target. She was ideal for what I had in mind.

James was an ideal match for her. Both were gym rats and worked out several times a week. She was an accountant and he owned a gun store in Alton. As a couple, they were perfect for my plan, but I was reluctant to involve her in my crazy scheme.

At one of our recent barbecues with them, I broached the notion of my plot.

"Well, Rob, who would you persuade to take on this trick?" James asked.

"It would have to be someone I totally trust to actually do it, and to tell no one," I answered.

"Aren't you taking a chance telling us?"

"You and I have become close friends, these past few years. I think that I can trust you both."

"What would this couple have to do?" Mary asked.

"They would have to develop a scheme to entice the burglar to break into their house when they were there."

"I'm not sure I understand, Rob. How does that work?" Mary asked.

"We are sure that whoever has been breaking into these homes, scouts them out first. It's part of his MO.

"The woman would be the lure. She would begin by partially undressing in the evening with the bedroom shades not drawn. She would have to set a pattern of this behavior."

"That's asking a lot, Rob," James said.

"I know, I doubt that I can find a woman willing to do that given the inherent potential danger."

"Oh, Rob, I don't know about that. I might be willing if it helps to catch this guy," Mary responded.

"Mary, be careful," Anne interjected.

"Plus, Mary, I'm not sure I would like you to show your things to a stranger," James snapped.

"I'm not asking you two to do this."

"Well, maybe you should, Rob. I think we would be ideal for this."

"Mary, you need to think a lot more about this for a while," I cautioned.

"I don't want to put Mary in the hands of a killer, Rob."

"You wouldn't be, James."

"Why would he come to a house with a man there?"

"He wouldn't. That's why the man could not appear to be living there."

"How does that happen?"

"I want a man in that house at all times, but he can't be visible. He has to stay hidden. He has to be there 24/7 until the pervert strikes."

"Where would this plan happen?" James asked.

"There is a house at #33 Lake Drive Circle in the Northwest section, which is owned by Konrad McCray. He has moved to another city. I have spoken to him about renting the house for a few months."

"Rob, have you lost it, Man? How are this guy and this woman showing off her butt going to pull off this charade for a few months? It's craziness."

"Look, it's been more than four months since he struck

last. His ability to continue to hold out is dying fast. He will strike soon. I can't tell you how soon, of course, but my gut says soon."

"So, if we do it, what is my role?" James asked.

"The reason I want a man with good firearm knowledge and ability is to stop this guy cold. If he can be held until we arrive, fine, if not…"

"So, if I were to kill him…"

"This is a 'stand your ground' state. The DA would not bring charges; just don't empty a magazine into him."

"If I were to agree to this, Rob, there is only one man I would trust; it is James," Mary said.

"I don't know about this, Rob. We'll get back to you."

"Again, guys, I am not asking you to do this. I may never find anyone to agree to help, but…"

Chapter Thirty

Days later, to my great surprise, James and Mary called and agreed to the scheme. I asked them both to my home again to further discuss the details.

"I want to reduce any possibility that things could go wrong. I want to make this as foolproof as we can," I explained.

"What do we need to do?" Mary asked.

"First, I know you that you appreciate this is dangerous. I wouldn't ask if I felt there was any other way. I don't feel very good about involving you, but you are the only ones I can trust. There can be no remuneration for what you are doing. Even afterward, there can be no publicity, no book deals, nothing. Can you agree to that?"

"We both do, Rob."

"Second, there can be no discussion of any Augusta Police involvement. I am not worried for myself, but I don't want the Department dragged down because of me."

"Does this suspect carry a firearm?"

"We don't think so. Both victims of his attacks said that he threatened them with a knife, not a gun, but we don't know for certain. In any event, from the victims' statements, he was preoccupied with other things in his hands."

"What if he does try to use a gun and I have to shoot him? Will the DA press charges?" James asked.

"It's possible; I will be pressuring him to respect your right to defend yourselves. He knows what this creep did to a few of the residents in Glendale."

"What's next for us to do?" Mary probed.

"As I said earlier, I have spoken to the home owner. I've asked him to install a louvered door in place of the solid one leading to the walk-in closet of the master bedroom. That is key to this setup because you will be in there every night after Mary turns out the bedside lights.

"There will be a light switch installed in the closet so that you can switch those lights back on when you need. From the closet, you will be able to make out shadows moving about."

"What do I do when he comes into the room?" James probed.

"You maintain your cool, James. You've been baptized under fire before. You are the reason this plan can work. I don't believe I could trust anyone else to do this."

"And I wouldn't do this if James wasn't backing me up," Mary added.

"I can't thank you two enough. We must stop this guy. What you will do is critical," I said trying to encourage them, "We will get this done. If there was any other way, I would do it myself."

"What are the next steps, Rob?" James asked.

"By the end of next week, I want you to move into the cottage at #33 Lake Drive Circle. The owner has assured me that the work he and I have discussed will be complete."

"How do I move in without anyone learning about it?"

"That's easy, James, you will be one of the moving

guys. Four of you will move in the furniture; three of you will leave. If our suspect is keeping an eye on the move-in, he will probably not notice the difference. You will all wear the same uniforms. Your clothes, firearms, ammo, and anything else you need will be part of the move.

"Mary, you will be in and out of the cottage pretending to direct where you want things to be placed in the cottage. Again, if he is casing the move-in, I want him to see you."

"Do I need to wear a revealing outfit?" Mary asked.

"Not too revealing, Mary."

"I agree, James, I don't think that's necessary. The other victims weren't soliciting his activities. You need time to get settled into a routine. Although I want this over as soon as possible, you must have time to acclimate to the new surroundings. Further, James has to practice what he will do when the time comes."

"I understand. I will be sexy, but not flagrant about it."

"Good. Once you are moved in, James, you cannot be seen by anyone. You need to sleep in the daytime; I know it will take some getting used to.

"The small bedroom next to the master bedroom will be ideal. The windows are high enough so that one passing by cannot see into it. You must be awake and sharp during the night."

"How long will this take, Rob?" James probed again.

"I am hoping within two weeks it will be over. One thing the owner has done for us is to place ads in the Augusta paper looking for a renter for his cottage. The suspect seems to be aware of changes in the neighborhood so the ad may help."

"Does the owner know what's going on in his cottage?" Mary asked.

"I've told him as much as I can, which is not much. Actually, I have not really spoken to him. My inquiries and requests for changes to the cottage were done through a third party whom I will not name."

"You've really thought this one through, Rob."

"I have, James; I don't want anything to go wrong. I hope we can bring this guy to trial, but he is secondary to my concerns for you two. If he is injured, so be it, but I care what happens to you. Do you still want to go through with this?"

"Of course, Rob, we would like to help in any way we can to bring this murderer down," Mary said.

"You two are exceptional. I can think of no others who would be willing to undertake this. Thank you, Folks. I lose sleep over this. I can assure you."

"Is there anything else we should know?"

"Yes, it's how you will play your part, Mary."

"And that is?"

"The master bedroom faces the rear of the cottage. The outside area is dark with no external lighting. I recommend that we use low wattage bulbs in the bedside lamps; enough to read by, but low enough to provide some muted light in the room. I'll have some in the lamps for you.

"When you undress, leave the blinds open enough so

that anyone looking in would be able to see what you are doing. As you say, we don't want to be flagrant about this. You need to undress only to the point you feel comfortable. Don't do anything that bothers you."

"I will do what I normally do at our home, Rob. I will not face the window; I will have my nightgown within reach so that I can slip it on. He will only see by backside. Okay?"

"Perfect, James will be in the closet by the time any lights are turned on."

"How do I become one of the moving guys?" James asked.

"I know the owners. Sometimes, people of the force moonlight. Since this was a special request to move you, I volunteered you as someone who would help for this move. Mary will ask to have you remain to unpack some boxes. That does happen sometimes, so that will not be a red flag for them."

"Anything else?" Mary asked.

"Yes, the moving truck will be ready on Thursday of this week. Please be ready."

"I've already told my store manager to cover for me while I'm on 'vacation' for three weeks," James replied.

"Excellent! Mary, you are planning to continue working, yes?" I asked.

"Yes, I asked about vacation, but this is a bad time of year for me to take leave."

"It's too far to commute to Alton, how will you be able

to manage the work?"

"The same way I do when I'm in Alton, Rob. If I have internet access, I can do my job."

"Okay, Mary, that's good. Folks, I have a couple of last important details we must consider. Let's review three possible scenarios. Are you ready?"

"We're as ready as we'll ever be, Rob."

"First scenario: the guy comes into the bedroom. James, you will flip on the bedroom light while stepping out of the closet. You must have your firearm ready to fire. You tell the perp to get on the floor, then tie-wrap his hands behind his back, if possible, but don't put yourself in danger. Mary will phone 911. My detective, Ray Brown, will come to the scene and take charge.

"Second scenario: the guy comes into the room. Again, you will flip on the bedroom light while stepping out of the closet with your firearm ready to fire. You tell him to get on the floor, but he starts to rush you. You fire to wound him, not kill him, if possible. You need to quickly check the condition of the guy. Again, don't put yourself in danger. If necessary, tie-wrap his hands behind his back. Mary calls 911.

"What you do next is very important. I cannot stress it enough. After the guy is down, you both move to the front porch. You must put your firearm on the floor of the porch, at least five feet away from you. It is crucial that the firearm is placed away from you when the police arrive.

"Mary will stay on the line with the 911 dispatcher until

the police get there. Again, Ray Brown, will come to the scene and take charge.

"Third scenario: Mary senses that someone is watching her. After shutting off the lights, but the man never enters the house. You do nothing. You do not leave the house to try to find him. The suspect must enter the cottage and try to do something to Mary before you can fire any round at him. This is critical. You must remember that."

"I've got it, Rob."

"One more thing: call my cell phone every morning at eight o'clock for a check-in. Last: if you want to stop this at any time, let me know. I will understand. None of this is worth having you hurt or upset. You have to be willing and able."

"We will finish this, Rob," Mary said.

"Thank you both for your courage. I think we have covered everything we need to. Any last questions?"

"No, let's get this over with," James said.

"Now we have to wait until the suspect makes his move. Thank you both."

If West or, God forbid, Roy made his move, I felt we were ready.

Chapter Thirty-One

The first week passed slowly. Each morning I received my call from James or Mary. The report was irritatingly brief: nothing occurred the night before. I was beginning to think that our suspect somehow knew of the plan.

I had not told James and Mary the name of the suspect, West, as I felt it would have made them more nervous if they knew that I thought that there was more than one suspect. I needed them to be calm and ready to act at any moment.

One thing, which I hoped would not occur, was that our suspect might burgle the house in the daytime. If he did, the whole plan would be a waste of time and money. Worse, we were not certain that the burglar and killer were the same, so the plan could possibly fail anyway. This had been my detectives' concern from the start of this investigation, but the call I received on Tuesday morning of the second week erased those doubts.

"Rob, I think our plan is working. Last evening when I was undressing, I got this eerie feeling. You know, the kind of sensation that makes the hair on your neck feel as though it is standing up," Mary reported.

"Were you able to see anything?"

"No, my back was to the window, but when I did turn slightly toward it, I think I saw some movement of the bush outside."

"Did you alert James?"

"Yes."

"What happened next, Mary?"

"As I said, at first, I doubted myself, but when I turned away from the window, the feeling returned. There wasn't any breeze that night, so I know what I felt was true."

"I know this sounds daring, but I continued undressing knowing that 'he' was watching me. I decided to give him something to really see. Not a full frontal, Rob, but he knows what I have."

"You are special, Mary, but be careful. You've got him going now. It's only a matter of time before he acts. Were you able to see anything about him?"

"No, he probably hides behind the bush there."

"So, even facing the window you couldn't see anything?"

"Not really, Rob, it's very dark out back. James went out this morning to see if there were any footprints, but there weren't."

"Thank you, Mary, speak to you tomorrow. Can you put James on the line?"

"Here he is."

"James, what the hell are you doing? You can't go outside, ever. You could kill this whole plan."

"I'm sorry, Rob, I didn't think."

"Okay, don't do it again. I hope he didn't see you."

"I won't, Rob."

"James, Mary alerted you with the sign, yes?"

James and Mary had agreed upon a sign to alert James if the suspect was peeping in the window. The sign was that she would pick up her nightgown and drop it to the floor as though it had slipped from her hand.

"She did. When it happened, I felt my stomach tighten."

"That's good, James. Remember you can do nothing until the suspect enters the house."

"I know, Rob, we've spent enough time discussing this possible situation."

"Good man. Okay, I'll talk to you tomorrow morning unless…"

"Unless he comes into the cottage. I'll be ready, Rob."

"Good, get some sleep."

"Yes, I will."

I received morning calls for the next two days. I was beginning to feel that James' indiscretion had blown the whole plan.

My cell phone rang at two fifteen the next morning. I rolled over and answered it to hear, "Rob, this is James, get over here right away. I shot him!"

"I'm on my way. I'll be there in five minutes. Do as I said and go to the porch with the firearm as I told you. Don't panic. Has Mary called 911?"

"She has. We're on our way to the porch."

"Good, see you shortly."

Soon afterward, I got another call, "Chief, this is Ray, you need to get over to 33 Northwest in Glendale. We just got a 911 call. Our intruder has struck. I'm on my way out there."

"Okay, Ray, I'm on my way. I'm close to Glendale."

As I drove to the address, I hoped that West had finally made the fatal mistake. Then I began to worry that Roy may be the one who had been shot.

My mind could not accept that one friend had had to shoot another, closer friend. Why, Roy, why did you have to make me do this? I could feel my stomach tightening. I wanted to pull over and vomit, but I controlled myself.

When I reached the cottage, the ambulance and Ray had scarcely arrived. James and Mary were on the porch as I had instructed them.

James had put the 9mm Ruger on the table. Both had tears in their eyes. James hands were trembling. Their courage had faded once the deed had been done.

"Where is the person located?" I heard Ray ask.

"In the master bedroom," James answered.

Ray and a patrolman went into the house. When Ray gave the all clear signal, the EMT's rushed past us.

Moments later, Ray and the EMTs came back to the porch.

"We see blood on the carpet by the bed, but there's no body there. What's going on?" Ray said with obvious concern.

"What? Stay here James," I ordered.

Ray and I went into the bedroom. Beside the bed, a large puddle of blood stained the carpet. A bloody drip trail led from there through the open door to the patio in the back. Bloody fingerprints, now drying, were on the door above the latch handle.

"I'll take the statements from James and Mary," I ordered as we walked back to the porch.

"Chief, you know these people?" Ray asked while slipping the Ruger into an evidence bag.

"I do, Ray."

"Chief, what is going on here?"

"I'll bring you up to speed later. Get a search started. We need to find him. He can't have gotten very far."

"Right, Chief, but there is no lighting out there."

"Do the best you can. Get some help from the patrol unit here."

With that, I returned to James and Mary. I took them to my cruiser and said, "Okay, Folks, tell me what happened."

"Rob, this is the first person I ever killed," James said with pain in his voice.

"James, try to relax. Just tell me what happened," I responded as Ray walked to the porch to retrieve the gun.

"Rob, it was just two in the morning; Mary had been in bed for several hours. I was…"

"I lay down around 9:30 and read for a while before turning off the lights. Before I knew it, I was asleep," Mary interrupted.

"Okay, what happened next, James?"

"I thought I saw a shadow move by the bedroom doorway. Whoever it was made no noise. Then I saw him approach the side of the bed. Before I knew it, he had jumped on top of Mary. She started to scream; he clamped his hands on her mouth.

"In a split second, or so it seemed, he had flipped her on her stomach; that's when I switched on the bedroom lights and pushed open the closet door."

"The guy froze for a second; I fired two rounds into him. I don't know where I hit him for sure. I could see one wound starting to bleed from his chest area. The other must have hit him in his arm."

"Okay, James, what did you do next?"

"When the guy got hit, he tumbled onto the floor. I went over to him and he wasn't moving. I assumed he was dead. Mary grabbed her phone. Then we both went to the porch as you told us."

"Is that when you called 911?"

"Yes, I was so frightened that I almost couldn't dial the phone."

"You both did fine. I'm so sorry that I had to involve you. Detective Brown is searching for him now. We'll find him. I'm going to have a patrol car take you to the hospital for a check, and then to the station for your formal statements. Another detective, Alissa Riley, will be there for you. I'll be around shortly."

"Are we in trouble, Rob?" James asked.

"James, it is what we have to do to document what happened. It's standard procedure. We must notify the DA. Just answer any questions that Alissa has for you."

"Does she know of the plan?"

"She does. I called her after you called me. She and Brown knew about my plan, but they didn't know that we had implemented it. They were against it from the start. I Relax, if you can. I will get there as soon as I'm able to."

I hadn't asked James and Mary for a description of the suspect because I knew that we would find him. From the blood scene, and James' description of the wounds, he would have to go to a hospital or die.

I knew I would have to face Detective Brown over my plan, since I had specifically not informed him. When the trouble hit, I didn't want him or Alissa involved. He was too close to retirement. Alissa was only informed at the last minute.

Chapter Thirty-Two

"Chief, it's just too dark to follow any blood trail. It looked as though he turned right from the patio as he walked or crawled away. The wind is picking up out there, scattering his trail so I can't really say which direction he took," Ray said as soon as he saw me.

"That's too bad. We don't want him to get away, but the guy who shot him is sure he is carrying a slug in his chest area. He won't get far."

"Probably not, we did find a knife in the bedroom. You could gut a deer with it. It's razor sharp."

"So, he came to kill, did he?"

"Maybe, but that wasn't his MO with Newman. He used a knife to cut her clothes off her."

"Yeah, I remember. Anything else of interest?"

"Yeah, Chief, very interesting. We found a camera and tripod leaning by the back door. They'll be tagged, bagged and sent to the station for Forensics."

"Good work, Ray."

"Okay, Chief, now tell me who those two people are," Ray insisted.

"They are friends who I used to set up my sting to nail the suspect. I apologize for not telling you, Ray, but I think you can understand. If anything went wrong, I couldn't let your career be on the line."

"Did Alissa know?"

"I told her something was in the works, but I purposely left out any details so that she could reasonably say she had no knowledge of what I was talking about. I wanted her to be ready to take statements when needed. While you were outside, I phoned her and sent the two to the station to meet her.

"You remember that I had said I was thinking about a way to capture our killer, but I didn't want you two involved with the details. This whole mess is on my plate. Now, I have to find a way to protect my friends who were part of my plan.

"So, who are they?"

"James Mills and Mary Adams. They are engaged to each other. James is an expert marksman. What happened tonight was a case of nerves; he didn't shoot straight, thankfully."

"So, you set this up and didn't let me know?"

"I couldn't, Ray, you are too close to retirement. I didn't want to spoil that for you. Actually, I didn't want to involve either of you."

"So, you set up a trap for your friend, Roy, and…"

"It may not be Roy. We agreed that West was the most logical suspect, remember?"

"I do, but my money is on Roy. Shall we send a cruiser to Roy's house?"

"Not yet, it will be light in an hour. Get some patrolmen and try to pick up this guy's trail. Again, he can't have gone far. He was losing a great deal of blood."

"I have a suggestion, Chief. We need to visit each cottage in the Northwest and Southwest sections this morning. Somebody may have noticed something."

"I agree, Ray, can you get that moving?"

"I will as soon as I return to the station."

"Witness statements may be needed if we are able to bring the creep to justice. If it is Roy or West, we won't have any trouble finding them."

"Chief, West's cottage is one we will visit first this morning. I know you hope it's him; for your sake, I hope you're right."

"I'll wait for your report, Ray. I'm going to the station to see Alissa."

Later that morning, Ray called me. His excitement was obvious.

"We found him, Chief!"

"That's great news, Ray. I knew it was West all along."

"I'm sorry Chief, but you are wrong. It is your friend."

Ray's news felt like a stab to my heart. "Roy, Roy, Roy, you stupid, stupid fool. What the hell happened to you?" I cried to myself.

"Oh, no, Ray. Is he dead?"

"He is; he reached cottage number 41 in the Northwest section. He must have stumbled along the back yards of the cottages. I was wrong last evening; he went north along the lake from where he was shot. He was just inside the back door. It was there he bled out."

"How did he get inside the door?"

"We can't tell yet, but there is blood everywhere."

"Do you know whose cottage it is?"

"We talked to West. Coincidentally, the cottage at number 41 is next to his. He says that the owner doesn't stay there very often. In fact, he's never met him. He only knows that some nights he sees lights in the cottage go on and off. West said he knocked on the door one time, but whoever it was, didn't answer. He can't ever remember seeing him coming or going to the cottage."

"Ray, maybe, the lights are programmed to cycle. You know, fool people into thinking someone is home. Since it's a crime scene, get the Forensics' folks to search the house."

"They are already here, Chief. I can tell you they are finding piles of women's panties, bras and other underwear here. You wouldn't believe the amount; neatly folded and boxed up. There must be twenty large boxes full. Plus, there are literally tons of photographs of the dead man, nude and are disgusting."

"What? The pervert lives there?"

"It must be."

"Ray, you said the dead man is, was a friend of mine. It's not Roy, is it?"

"No, Chief, it's not Roy."

"Thank, God, but who is it, Ray? Why did you mislead me?"

"Sorry, Chief, I didn't mean to do that."

"I have a lot of friends in Augusta. Well, they are really acquaintances, so why did you say a friend?"

"I'm not sure, Chief, but his face looks familiar; that's

why I said it was a friend of yours. I know I've seen him before, but I've never been good with faces, especially this one now. It's contorted with a lot of blood on his face."

"You gave me a hell of a scare, Ray. I thought you meant Roy."

"No, I sent a cruiser over to his house. He's fine, pissed off at being woken up, but fine."

"Thanks, Ray, what a relief. Now we've got to identify this dead guy."

"We've opened up the garage, Chief. There is a Mercedes parked there."

"Get the registration on the car."

"We checked that. Hang on, Chief, here it is. It belongs to a Marvin Evans."

"Okay, Ray, things we know are beginning to come together. I will have Alissa check the county records for ownership of the cottage. I think we are almost there."

After my call with Ray finished, thoughts began to swirl in my mind. The name Marvin Evans was familiar, but it wasn't recent. I needed to call Anne.

Chapter Thirty-Three

"Hi, Anne; hate to bother you at work."

"No bother, Rob. I have been worried ever since the call last night. Are you okay?"

"I'm fine, Love. We got a huge break in this murder case last night. The guy is dead, I'm sorry to say."

"I can tell from your voice that it wasn't Roy, am I right?"

"No, thank God, it wasn't Roy."

"Who was it?"

"We're not sure yet. The guy crawled to a cottage in the Northwest section. The cottage belongs to a Marvin Evans. Do you remember that name from our past? It seems familiar, but I'm not sure."

"Whew, Rob, that was a long time ago. The only Evans I can remember was Maryanne Evans. I'm not certain, but wasn't her father's name, Marvin?"

"What, Anne? Maryanne? Abner's father-in-law?"

"I could be wrong, Rob."

"No, I think you're right. Abner's father-in-law. Thanks, Anne, you've been a great help. Love you."

I immediately called Ray.

"Has the coroner been out?"

"Yes, the body has been taken to the morgue."

"I was going to run out to the Glendale cottage, but I'll head for the morgue instead."

"I can meet you there, Chief."

When the sheet was pulled back to reveal the face of the

dead man, I was stunned. It could not be! But it was. My friend of so many years lay on that cold stainless slab. It was then I realized how much I had been fooled. No, how easily I had allowed myself to be fooled.

Was Roy right? Was life really a zero-sum game? What goes around; is what comes around? I had betrayed a friend. A friend had betrayed me. Is that how life works?

I knew that I had to make several calls, the first particularly agonizing.

"Maryanne, this is Rob Connor. I have very bad news."

"What is that?"

"Abner has died."

The response from Maryanne was unexpected.

"How did it happen?" she asked with not a hint of emotion in her voice.

"He was shot burglarizing a house and attempting to hurt a woman here in Augusta."

"What? I don't believe it, Rob."

"Maryanne, I can't believe it either. It breaks my heart. He was such a friend back then."

"You know, Rob, that Abner and I have been estranged for several years?"

"I didn't, Maryanne. Anne and I have invited Abner and you to dinner several times over the past year. He said that you were always busy with your work, so we stopped inviting."

"Before we split, Abner's habits were becoming very strange. I couldn't and wouldn't put up with them. He finally moved out."

"Where was he staying?"

"He had an apartment in Portland. I moved back to Bards Crossing to be closer to my mother. My father died two years ago and left me a cottage in Augusta. We used to vacation there for a few weeks a year. I went there for the last time shortly after he died. We have been thinking about selling it, but my mother seems reluctant to part with it."

"I hate to tell you this, Maryanne, but Abner has been using the cottage as a base for his activities."

"God, Rob, what else has he done?"

"He tortured and murdered a young woman. He has paid for it with his life."

"I can't believe it! I am so sorry to hear that, Rob. He changed; I don't know why."

With that, the call ended. Another person betrayed. For me, the case was closed, but not over. My friend, Abner had used his father-in-law's cottage as a base of operation and storage of his demented trophies. He had paid for his evil ways with his life.

The second call to the FBI Section Chief, Patrick Kelly, in Portland was short.

Within a couple of hours, the Section Chief and several agents arrived in Augusta. The usual "we know better than you" attitude was immediately apparent. Kelly believed that their agent had been brutally murdered. They would get to the bottom of this and arrest the killer. No one gets away with that. It was unbelievable that a decorated agent was being accused of such heinous crimes.

The state bureau of investigation promptly intervened to ensure a true, unbiased enquiry. I was to be a bystander in the process.

The long process of questions and depositions began. Of course, the whole covert sting operation, which I had fathered had to come into the open. Although I had acted in the best interests of the Augusta citizens, my methods were illegal. At least I had shielded my detectives.

It was inevitable that I would lose my position as Chief of Police. I had no regrets. A murderer had been caught, but it would take some time before everyone accepted that.

At the end of the finger pointing, it was the self-damning evidence that proved our case. The digital camera held the last moments of Jane Newman being raped, beaten and strangled. Other photos showed the malicious raping of Abigail Stevens and the torture of Linda Savage.

The DA agreed to not pursue any charges against James and Mary when the convincing photographic evidence proved that Agent Abner Smith was the killer of Jane Newman. There was no doubt.

To this day, I regard James and Mary as two of my true friends, although after it was all over, they moved out west and we weren't in contact much anymore. I was ashamed to have involved them in my scheme.

I spoke to Kelly in my office to understand the evidence Abner said existed to implicate Roy.

"Agent Kelly, I was told by Agent Smith that you were

working an important case here in Augusta, actually in the Glendale section. He said that he had an informant who was certain that one of our residents was the suspect we needed to arrest. Is that true?"

"The only thing I will say is that we are, but there is no informant who knew anything about your Glendale murderer."

These cases had destroyed three innocent women's lives, shredded the myth of safety in the Glendale District and ended my two longtime friendships. Abner's death meant that only my memories of our carefree days when we were young and dreaming of conquering the world would live on. I could try to remember him as kind and caring, but that was a world long ago lost. In truth, he had become a terrible danger to all that I held right and dear.

As for Roy, he and I never reconnected as we had before the trouble. That I had let him down by not believing in him would never leave my conscience. Any time that Roy and I met after Abner's death was cold. We only met a few times, and they were without meaningful conversation or emotion. We finally agreed never to meet again.

Over dinner, Anne and I talked about the strange, sad events that trapped us and our two friends.

"Anne, I can't understand what went so wrong with Abner. What makes a man change so drastically?"

"I hate to say this, Rob, but I have never felt comfortable with Abner even when we were in high school. There was just something about him."

"You never said anything to me."

"I know; I didn't want to hurt you. He was your best friend."

"Well, maybe you should have, Anne."

"What I do feel bad about happened recently."

"What do you mean?"

"Well, you remember when Abner was stayed here while we went away?"

"Yeah, what about it?"

"Do you remember that I said something about my underwear being missing?"

"I remember that, but you said you weren't sure anything was taken."

"Rob, I was absolutely sure. I had put several things into the hamper to be washed when I got home. When we returned, all of them were gone. It could have only been Abner who took them."

"Wasn't Roy in the house during that time also?"

"He was, the following week. I did the same thing as I had done when Abner watched the house; I left soiled laundry. When we got back, Roy had done the laundry, bless his heart, but my underthings were washed, folded and put away. No, it was not Roy."

"Why didn't you tell me?"

"At the time, Rob, things in the District were becoming such a problem. You weren't telling me any details about what was happening. I thought if I started saying what I thought, it would only make things worse for you. In retrospect, I should have."

"I understand; it probably wouldn't have made much difference because I would have found it too hard to believe."

With that conversation, Anna and I let the matter rest. We agreed that we would not talk about Roy or Abner because of the pain I felt.

One day several years later, a terrible 911 call to the station put an end to the story of Roy Hepburn. Alone, he had taken his life, and in some ways, he had taken a part of mine.

Alissa found a note beside the body of Roy.

Dear Faithless Friend,

When you find this letter, I will be gone. The years we knew each other and called each other friends are too painful to think about. That friendship ended when you showed your true colors. You never defended me. I know you told your goons to do whatever they could to make me confess, but they failed. I was innocent.

Your transparent effort to invite me over to smooth things over was so bad that I began to hate you for it. You had no evidence, but you were judge, jury, and executioner. A fine cop you have become. I was a much better friend to you that you ever were to me.

The pain of living without Heidi has now forced me to do what I should have done years ago. At least I die knowing that justice has been served for all those that wronged me and my real friends. I can go to my grave

knowing that you were wrong, wrong, wrong about me.
Your so-called friend Abner made you look the fool you
are.

I have changed my will so you can have a good life on
my dime. I hope you rot in hell.

I go to Heidi in peace.

Roy

I attempted to determine if Roy had inflicted vigilante justice on those who had harmed Heidi, his first wife, and John Goldie's killer. I wanted to clear my nagging doubts. Was it just fate that shadowed Roy? But I knew that it was unknowable. Roy was a good man. I just knew it. Was it my fate to have two good friends who ultimately died by my indirect hand?

A few months later, I received a letter from an attorney representing Roy's estate who stated that Roy had executed a last will and testament several years ago. Roy directed his estate's considerable disbursement to several charities as well as to me.

I was to inherit an insignificant sum of money; thirty silver dollars. No doubt that Roy meant to equate me with Judas and his betrayal of Christ. As always, he was right.

It has been many years since that fateful time in Augusta. The memory of my friend Roy and my part in his anguish persists to this day. It was dreadful for me to admit that I had contributed to his declining health, my self-interested role that drove him to his ultimate relief from pain.

As Anne said many times to comfort me, "There were many victims. Roy was inadvertently involved in the crime investigation. The women who were tortured and raped. Jane Newman who was killed. You, who had to do your sworn duty. You had to stop the killing. You cannot blame yourself."

Amazingly, I did not lose my position at the Augusta Police Force, but the constant reminders of what had occurred pushed me to retire early.

I am constantly reminded by the unknown sage who wrote: "Conscience is a cur that will let you get past it, but that you cannot keep from barking."

My conscience will never be clear.

These days I am alone, living in a small apartment back in Bards Crossing where I started out. My dearest friends, Mom, Anne, Roy, and Abner are all gone. My nights are filled with thoughts, "what ifs," that could have changed the course of my life. Today I have no "true friends" and it is the "others" who call daily to see if I am well. Perhaps I misjudge them.

About the Author

Jon A Sanborn, writing as J A Sanborn, has written six mystery novels: *The Lost Cipher, The Orion Factor, Death Comes to Ely, The Stillwater Incident, Of Friends and Others, and Recollections – An Olio of Short Stories.*

The author holds a BS degree in chemistry and a Ph.D. in computational chemistry from the University of Massachusetts Amherst.

He is a U.S. Navy veteran who served in an antisubmarine squadron, VS-34, aboard the antisubmarine aircraft carrier, USS Essex, CVS-9, at the peak of the Cold War during the Cuban Missile Crisis in 1962.

He has had a career spanning thirty years in various management positions in high technology corporations as well as fifteen years in academic settings teaching chemistry.

After retirement, he formed Swift River Publishing to provide publishing services for his own novels, and for people who have written manuscripts and wish to have them published at modest cost.

He has had a lifetime interest in physics, chemistry, ciphers, codes, and mystery stories: fact and fiction.

He and his wife live in Savannah, Georgia with a spoiled tuxedo cat.